DEPRESSION OR BUST

"Son," the president said. "What in the name of Moses is going on in this country?"

Weigand, his pipe clenched tightly between his teeth, said, "Mr. President, it's a Depression."

"A Depression?"

"Yes, sir."

"*What* is a Depression?"

"Well sir, I've been reading up on it. We haven't had one since 1939. Before our time, of course. What usually happens is that businesses fold, millions of people lose their jobs and go on relief—"

"All right, I think I get the idea. But how do you get rid of them?"

Weigand had been afraid he was going to ask that. "That's a good question. . . ."

World traveler, expert observer of the human condition, Mack Reynolds has been a world famous Science Fiction writer for more than two decades. In fact, of all the writers published in the leading SF magazines, *Galaxy* and *If,* a poll conducted among the readers put the stories of Mack Reynolds consistently higher than any other. Perhaps it is because his stories have an uncanny way of discussing *now* the questions that will concern everyone ten or twenty years later.

Mack Reynolds is the author of more than two hundred SF short stories, novelettes and novels. Many of them have been published by Ace Books and more will be published in future months.

Depression or Bust

by
Mack Reynolds

WILDSIDE PRESS

Elements of this story have appeared in *Analog* Maga-
zine entitled DEPRESSION . . . OR BUST, EXPEDIT-
ER, and FAD. And in the *Magazine of Fantasy and
Science Fiction* entitled THE EXPERT.

DEDICATION

To Vance Packard
Who provided me with the amoeba of the idea while
suffering the Madrid Minuet, in Spain.

FOREWORD

*The way the computers checked back on it later, it all
began in the home of Marvin and Phoebe Sellers, 4011
Camino de Palmas, Tucson, Arizona. Marv Sellers, at 7:30
p.m., on a Friday in May was going over his income and
his outgo. It had taken him a good hour before he came
up with his history shaking conclusions.*

*"Phoebe," he said, "there can't be no other damn way of
working it out."*

*"How'd you mean, Marv?" She was heating up three
dinners, one Mexican, one Chinese, one Italian, in the
electronic cooker.*

*"That new deep freeze'll hafta go back. What the hell
was wrong with the old one?"*

*"Why, Marv, you know we had that old deep freeze
nearly onto three years. The new ones got a lot of improvements. It was into all the ads, on the Tri-Di and all."*

*"Old one wasn't even paid for yet," Marv said. "What
new improvements, for crissakes?"*

*"Well, the old one was colored white. Nobody has a
white deep freeze any more."*

*Marv said, "Anyway, we gotta send this one back to the
store. We just can't stretch out the payments, what with
the house and the car and the furniture and swimming
pool and that there vacation we took, rocket now, pay
later."*

"They ain't going to like that over to the store."

"Then they'll hafta lump it."

*Harry came around to Jim Wilkins and said, "Boss, I
just got a call from Marv Sellers. Says he can't keep up
the payments on that deep freeze he bought a few weeks
ago."*

*Jim Wilkins thought about it. He looked around the
shop, darkly. "Listen," he said. "Call the distributor up in
Phoenix and tell him to cancel that order for three new
freezers. We're overstocked in here."*

7

He turned on his heel and entered his small office. He was in a vile mood and the cancellation didn't help any. He sat down and thought about it for awhile, then switched on the phone and dialed.

When Bill Waters faded in one the screen, Wilkins said, "Listen, Bill, I'm going to have to postpone that Buick Cayuse air-cushion."

Waters argued for awhile. "I think you ought to reconsider. You realize these new models have nearly a thousand horses under the hood? And built low? Did you hear the one about the guy thought it was raining out but he was only parked under a policeman's horse?"

Jim Wilkins sighed and said, "See you later, Bill."

Bill Waters flicked off the screen and turned to his secretary. He said, "Balls."

"I beg your pardon?"

"You heard me. Miss Harding, write to the Denver office and cut back our allotment. Oh, two cars a month in each line."

"Gosh, Mr. Waters, all on account of one cancellation?"

He looked at her. "I can sense a trend. Jim Wilkins must be taking a beating in that appliance store of his. Cars'll be next. I don't want to be overstocked."

He sat there for awhile. Finally, he switched on the phone again and dialed. When the screen lit up, he said, "Frank, I've been thinking about that new house. I think we better shelve it for the time being."

Chapter One

Weigand Patrick slouched on through the door of Scotty's office, fumbling in his jacket pocket for his tobacco pouch. He slung one leg over the corner of her desk and began rubbing a quantity of the rough-cut in his left hand with the thumb of his right.

Scotty, without looking up from the paper she was perusing, said, "Get your ass off my desk."

Weigand Patrick let his eyebrows go up. "I beg your pardon?"

"Get your ass off my desk," she said.

Weigand said, "You're pleasantly red-headed, got pleasantly blue-green eyes, and are built like a brick outhouse. It's a criminal shame that as nice a chunk of meat as Scotty McDonald doesn't put out."

"You're the world's most inept seducer," Scotty told him. "Given any finesse at all, and you would have had me in bed months ago."

"I've been trying for years."

"I haven't had the time, until these past few months."

"You'll wake up, one of these days, so old and wrinkled nobody around'll want to lay you," Weigand Patrick told her.

"A fate worse than debt," she snorted, going back to her report.

He said plaintively, "You practically promised, back during the campaign."

"We were in too much of a rush those days," she said, not looking up.

"Every night you went to bed, didn't you? I was perfectly willing to go along."

"I went to bed to sleep."

"That's a hell of a thing to waste time on in bed."

Scotty said, "I suppose there's some purpose in you being here besides practicing what is without doubt the lousiest approach to deflowering an innocent virgin known to the history of seduction."

"Virgin yes, innocent, no. You are the least innocent virgin in the tradition of virginity," Weigand told her. "How about a date? I mean *the* date. Finally made up your mind. Screw your courage to the sticking place as old Lady Macbeth had it. You don't seem to realize that you're in your mid-twenties. Ten years shot to hell. Some three thousand six hundred and fifty rolls in the hay wasted."

He produced a corncob pipe from another jacket pocket and fingered the rubbed tobacco into it. He brought forth a kitchen match and struck it beneath the desk and held it over the tobacco.

She twisted her mouth skeptically. On her it looked fine, the mouth being wide and good. She said, "You want I should have started when I was fifteen?"

"When they're old enough, they're big enough and when they're big enough, they're old enough," Weigand recited. "*I* started when I was fifteen." His face took on an overdone nostalgia. "She was a healthy little minx who'd been at it for years, at the age of fourteen. We were necking on her back porch and she asked me if I had ever played Inspection."

"Inspection," Scotty said.

"That's right," Weigand nodded very seriously. "Derived, I suppose, from the military short-arm inspection. Well, you'll never believe this but——"

"Spare me," Scotty growled. "Listen, Weewee Patrick . . ."

He flinched at that. "You *promised*," he protested.

10

". . . what in the hell do you want?"

He took the pipe from his mouth. "Well, if you must know, the Sachem sent for me."

"Oh." She looked at a pad to the left of her typer. "It's not on here. He has Secretary Bollix scheduled for three o'clock."

Weigand looked at his watch. "What's a Secretary of the Interior compared to the Sachem's alter ego, his *eminence grise*, the power behind the throne?"

"Ha," she said. "If you're going in, you'd better get underway. He and Bollix are going to go over that latest Far-Out Society bit of his. Project Porpoise. They've finally got those poor porpoises to the point they can really communicate with them. So the project is to lick the world protein shortage, put the porpoises to work out in the oceans riding herd on tremendous schools of whales. Whale meat tastes like beef, so they say. Now I've heard everything."

He unslung his leg from the desk, stood erect.

His voice had lost some of the banter. "How about the date, Scotty? It's in the cards. It's meant to be."

She looked at him and pursed her lips in thought. She took a deep breath. "All right," she said.

He whistled, a hiss of a whistle. "You mean it?"

"Yes. Yes, I guess I mean it."

"At my apartment?"

"I suppose so," she sighed.

"Whew! When? I'll have champagne. I'll have the caterers bring in the most elaborate . . ."

"Tonight," she said ruefully. "If it's not tonight, I'll talk myself out of it again. Why don't you ask me to marry you?"

"Why buy a cow, when milk's so cheap?" he said earnestly, as though really wanting to know. "Besides, you wouldn't want to marry me. I'd be a lousy provider.

11

I'm so improvident I can go into a revolving door and come out two dollars the poorer."

"Get the hell out of here," she growled at him. "You'll have Old Chucklehead on your neck. When he summons someone on his staff, he vaguely expects them to show up—sooner or later."

Weigand headed for the sanctum sanctorum. "He's already probably forgotten," he told her over his shoulder. "When I was a kid, my mother told me any American could become president, and I'm beginning to believe it. Now, don't forget, tonight's the night."

"I won't forget," she said. "It's probably the biggest mistake I've ever made."

"Bring a sleezy nightgown," he said, his hand on the doorknob. "No, on second thought you won't need it."

"What is it Chief?" Weigand said.

"Sit down, Son," Horace Adams told him, and before the other had lowered himself into one of the heavy leather chairs, "You find more time than I can to keep your ear to the ground. What in the name of Moses is happening in Cleveland? In fact, what's happening everywhere?"

"Why particularly Cleveland?"

The president took up a report and waved it. "We just got this hurry-up call asking for financial assistance to keep their soup kitchens going. What's a soup kitchen?"

Weigand Patrick reached for his tobacco pouch, even as he said, "Actually, not a very good term, under the circumstances. It goes back in time. What's happened in Cleveland is that they have this emergency food program. Those on their uppers can request free meals from the city."

"Is it that bad in Cleveland?"

"I'm afraid it is, Mr. President. And this project is just too much for them. You see, they tied it in with another program, to come to the relief of some of the delivery services, trucking concerns and so forth that were having a bad time. So instead of having to stand in line, at the soup kitchens, the food is delivered to each home."

"Well, what's the crisis?"

Weigand Patrick was packing his corncob. "Evidently, those on relief rebelled against the diet. Everybody's weight-conscious these days. They lit into City Hall demanding a low carbohydrate, high protein diet. You know, shrimp, steak, asparagus, artichokes, avocados, that sort of thing. Elections were coming up, so the city father capitulated."

For the moment, President Adams was in his own field of understanding. He said, "Well, that makes sense."

Patrick shrugged, searching for matches in several pockets. "Yes, sir. But the city treasury was already low, all taxes and other city income being down. Consesequently, they're calling on the Federal government for aid."

"Craminently!" the president snapped. "Don't they realize how much money we're going through as it is? Don't they realize how much it costs to be liberating Mozambique, containing Finland and conducting a police action in the Antarctic? Not to speak of the moon colony."

He picked up another report and waved it at his press secretary. "That's not all. That's not all by a damn sight. What's going on in Denver? They want money too."

"They ran out of local relief money and the unemployed drove on city hall."

"Drove on city hall?" the president scowled.

13

"Yes, sir. In the old days, people with a beef used to march on city hall, carrying banners and so forth. These days they drive."

"Oh." The president remained silent awhile, his face working as though in hard thought.

Which surprised Weigand Patrick. Presidents were not expected to be particularly bright anymore. This one had possibly the best public image, the most appealing Tri-Di television personality of all time, and a superlative hand shake.

"Son," he said finally. "What in the name of Moses is going on in this country?"

When Weigand got his pipe to fuming, he exhaled the smoke from his mouth and said, "Mr. President, it's a Depression."

"A Depression?"

"Yes, sir."

"*What* is a Depression?"

Weigand clicked the stem of his pipe against his teeth. "Well, sir, it's been a long time. I've been reading up on the matter the past few days. Checking it out. In the early days they'd call one a Panic or a Bust, but after a time they must have realized it didn't help get out of them by using that sort of terminology so they switched to Depression. Even that had too negative a connotation so after the big one, 1929 to 1939, they called them Recessions. Finally, some brain came up with Readjustment or Rolling Readjustment. But we haven't had a real blockbuster since 1939. Before our time, of course."

"But what *is* it?" In sudden irritation, the Chief Executive added, "What do you burn in that damned thing, soft coal?"

He slipped the pipe apologetically into a side pocket. "Well, sir, do you know the term geometric progression?"

The President had been involved in campus politics

14

at the time mathematics were being handed down, but he made a point of never admitting ignorance about anything.

Weigand Patrick understood the expression on the other's face. He said, "A geometric progression is when you go 2-4-16, uh, sixteen times sixteen would be, uh, 256. And so forth."

His ultimate superior was looking at him blankly.

Weigand shifted in his chair. "Well, sir, a depression is the opposite of that."

The other was still blank.

Weigand said, "Sir, take Los Angeles. It starts as a small city. Some people come out to retire, liking the weather. They have houses built. The contractors haven't enough construction workers to do the building so they offer premium wages and attract employees from back East. These like the looks of L.A. and decide to remain, which involves building more houses and apartment houses and stores to supply their needs. All this calls for more materials, cement plants, brickworks. It calls for more gasoline stations, more newspapers. More everything. A boom is on. More people arrive to get in on it. Money flows. Bars go up, nightclubs, nice restaurants. Boom begets boom. People making lots of money want luxuries. Car dealers go into business, swank hotels go up to house the businessmen coming to town.

"Little people get into the act too. They've twenty thousand dollars or so to invest in a small business. Largely, they go into things they know nothing about. A retired restauranteur starts a chicken farm. A retired farmer opens up a little restaurant specializing in Chinese food; he's a Swede. While they're building their restaurants or chicken farms, or Drive-In Tri-Di theatres, or whatever, they spark the boom still more."

The President said, "Yes, yes."

Weigand Patrick fished his pipe from his pocket unconsciously and pointed the stem at his superior. "Well, Mr. President, you can probably see it coming. The bust. The depression. Some of these little businesses fold. The empty buildings are up for lease. The construction workers go on unemployment insurance and cut back on their buying. They stop patronizing restaurants, beer joints and Tri-Di theatres. So a lot of these places fold or at least cut down their staffs, causing more unemployment. People stop buying new cars. The local agencies fold or cut back. People start leaving town to go back to living on small farms where they can at least grow their own gardens. Meanwhile, Detroit cuts back car production, which means cutbacks in steel and all the other things that go into cars. Detroit lays off a hundred thousand employees or so, and steel lays off the same. The farmers begin getting less call for their products and farm prices skid. The farmers stop buying everything from kitchen appliances to Joy perfume."

"All right, all right. I get the picture. It pyramids backwards," the President said.

Weigand winced but said, "That's about it, Chief."

The President's face worked in thought again, to the fascination of his press officer. Finally he said, "Why, this could be awful. Craminently, it's interfering with my Far-Out Society, the most fabulous society of all history."

Weigand Patrick clicked the stem of his pipe against his teeth. "Yes, sir, it'll do that. And all our aid programs. It's going to be difficult to keep shoveling all that money abroad."

His superior said plaintively, "How did they get rid of them in the past?"

Patrick had been afraid he was going to ask that. He

16

said, "Well, it's a good question. Roosevelt, who inherited the classic of all times, tried various things, most of which the Supreme Court kicked out. Like the NRA, which was supposed to mean National Recovery Act but, to most businessmen, meant Never Roosevelt Again. Then he figured on sending prices up by shooting pigs in the Middle West and pouring kerosene on potatoes up in Maine. He put all the juvenile delinquents into the CCC where he paid them to range around the woods supposedly planting trees and so forth. It's debatable whether they trampled more than they planted. Then he brought beer back."

"Brought beer back? Where'd it been?"

His press chief suppressed another wince. "He'd inherited Prohibition. But, of course, all that great experiment did was put the booze income into the pockets of the hoods, such as Al Capone. The government needed the taxes, so they brought back first beer and then liquor. That, of course, threw a lot of honest bootleggers out of work and they started robbing banks and kidnapping the few remaining citizens who had any money."

The President stared at him. "He sounds drivel-happy."

"Well, yes sir. At the time, a lot of people thought so. But, on the other hand, some thought him the greatest politician ever to come down the pike."

"Oh, they did, eh?" President Adams went through his thought processes. "I suppose there's a lot of political popularity to be won by a President who gets the nation out of a hole like this."

"Yes sir. I suppose there is. Roosevelt was reelected three or four times."

"Three or four times? That's illegal!"

"Roosevelt was pretty popular. He wowed them in California by paying the farmers to chop down their fruit trees."

The President was wide-eyed. "What did that accomplish?"

"Well, sir, it evidently made sense to Roosevelt and his brain trust. They wanted to send the price of fruit up. It seems as though there were some fifteen million unemployed and a lot of people hungry and . . ."

The President held up a hand. "Hold it, Son, you've lost me already. What was this about a brain trust?"

Weigand told him about the brain trust.

The President thought about it. "Hmmmmmm," he said. He thought about it some more.

Finally, he flicked a switch and said, "Fred?"

Fred Moriarty's voice came tinkling in. "Yes, Mr. President."

There was a petulant note in the chief executive's voice. "Why doesn't anybody ever tell me anything around here?"

Predictably, there wasn't any answer for that.

"I've decided I need a brain trust," the executive head of the United States of the Americas told him. "See about it."

"Yes, Mr. President. A brain trust."

The President flicked him off and turned back to Weigand. "What are you doing tonight?" he demanded.

Weigand said, "I've got a date, sir."

"Well, you can take her along."

Weigand looked at the other warily. "Yes, sir. To where?"

"To the party at the Soviet Complex Embassy."

"But I've been to a party at the Soviet Embassy. You eat caviar and smoked sturgeon and you drunk toasts to

18

peace and coexistence and togetherness until you fall down."

The President tapped the side of his nose two or three times with the forefinger of his right hand. It was his gesture indicating a sly performance on his part, with a connotation of inordinary wisdom being utilized. And it was one of the crosses his press secretary bore.

"That Nick Stroganoff, or whatever his name is . . ."

"Stanislov," Weigand said. "The new ambassador from the Soviet Complex."

"The CIA has passed on a couple of items about him. One, he doesn't hold his liquor any too well. Two, just before this appointment he was connected with their space program."

"So," Patrick said.

"So we want to know just how many men they plan to plant in their moon colony. If it's more than our eight, we're going to have to boost the size of our colony."

"I thought eight was all we needed. Two physicists, two astronomers——"

"Not if the Russkies send up more than eight." The Chief Executive shook a finger at his press secretary-cum-Man Friday. "A lot of people don't seem to realize, Son, that this race into space is still on. It all started back when Eisenhower was informed by the CIA that the Russkies planned to orbit an artificial satellite during that Geo-whatever-it-was year.

"Ike had some quick fellas on his team. Before the Russkies could announce their plan, *we* put on a special TV broadcast announcing that *we'd* orbit an artificial satellite in 1957. When the Russkies came out the next day and said they also were going to send one up, everybody laughed. It was our first space triumph."

Weigand Patrick said, "The trouble was, up to that

point we hadn't done any work on any such project."

"No, but we started right away. Of course, the son-of-a-bitchin Russkies got their sputnik up first. Then they had several other firsts, like the first dog up, and the first man, and the first orbit around the moon, the first woman, the first three men at a time, the first space walk."

The Chief Executive looked pained. "Finally we caught up. But you know, Son, somehow nobody—Eisenhower, Kennedy, Johnson, every administration since the space program began—nobody seemed to lay any plans for what we'd do once the moon was reached. The whole thing just stopped there."

He tapped himself on the chest modestly. "It was up to me. The space race continues. We've got to beat the Russkies by putting a bigger colony up there than they have."

"Yes, sir," Weigand sighed. "What's that got to do with me going to the May Day party at the Soviety Complex Embassy?"

The President shook a finger at him. "Strogonoff——"

"Stanislov."

"Whatever his name is. He'll get drenched. He practically has to. It's unpatriotic for a communist not to get smashed on May Day. You'll be around. You'll get the conversation around to the Moon colony. Maybe he'll drop a hint."

Weigand Patrick sighed again. "All right," he said.

Scotty's voice tinkled, "Mr. President, Secretary Bollix is here."

"All right, send him in." The President added vaguely to Weigand Patrick, "What in the name of Moses was it he wanted?"

Patrick unwound himself from his chair, fishing for pipe and tobacco pouch.

He said, "Your Far-Out Society. He probably wants to discuss that idea of yours, turning Wyoming into a National Park, putting all the remaining Indians in it, outfitted with their old equipment, bringing back the buffalo, and so forth."

The other's face lit up. "Ah, yes. The final solution of the National Park question. A big enough National Park to hold *all* the tourists. What do you think of the basic idea, Son?"

Patrick said unhappily, "I think the Indians would wind up scalping every car load of tourists that came through."

The President looked at him bleakly. "Let me know tomorrow how the party came out, Son."

Chapter Two

Marv Sellers came into the house from the back, the way he always did when he returned from work. He threw his hat on the kitchen table in disgust.

Old Sam looked up from where he sat in his rocker before the kitchen Tri-Di set and said, "What's wrong, boy?"

"Where's Phoebe?"

"She ain't home from work yet."

"Well, the contractor just laid me off. Me and eight of the other guys, fer crissakes."

"What happened?"

"Ahhh, the house we were going to be working on, the guy wanted it changed his mind. That Bill Waters over to the Buick agency. Business must be bad. Well, it's me for rocking-chair money for awhile. But you can't

21

make ends meet on a hundred a week unemployment insurance." He grunted disgust. "We'll hafta send back that new couch and easy chair Phoebe bought."

The old man said, "Lucky you still got the old ones out to the garage. Business bad, eh? I'll hafta talk that over with the boys in the park in the morning."

Marv opened the refrigerator for a plastic of beer. "Glad Phebe's working," he muttered. "Don't know how long it'll be before I get onta another job."

He flicked the top off the plastic with his thumb and took a long drink. He took the container away from his mouth and scowled at the imprinted label.

"What a slogan," he muttered. *"It's the Water.* It's the water, all right, but I'd rather have beer with some alcohol in it, fer crissakes."

Old Sam said, "You think beer'll ever come back? In the old days, we usta have beer with some body into it. It was kinda darker and you could taste the hops. It was richer and stronger. Then some New York wisenheimer come up with the discovery that maybe men drank more of the beer than dames but women bought it, usually down to the ultra-market. So he figures they better slant the ads to the womenfolks. So they come up with slogans like *light beer* and *dry beer.* What the hell's dry beer, and whatdaya want with light beer? Beer supposed to be rich. This stuff now, they can put it back in the horse. Folks now don't know Schlitz from Shinola."

"Sure, sure, gramps," Marv told him. "But you can't stand in the way of progress."

"Progress?" Old Sam said disgustedly. "Back when I was a youngster, we usta have a brew in Boston called Pickwick Ale. Yes, sir, the Poor Man's Whiskey, we called it. A nickel for a schooner. Three schooners and you was drenched. High we usta call it then. Three schooners and you was high as a kite, we called it. They usta have

22

free lunch in those days. Stuff like potato chips and cod fish balls."

"Best part of the cod fish," Marv muttered.

"What?"

"Nothing."

Phoebe came in and put down a heavy bag of groceries she was carrying, and Marv told her about being laid off.

She was her usual placid self.

"It's not important," she soothed him. "You'll have another job in no time at all. But meanwhile it takes a little thinking. We'll have to retrench, like they say." She laughed sourly. "This would have to happen on the night I wanted you to take me to June Perriwinkle's restaurant. Now I think I just better cook something here."

"Well, that's one good thing," Marv snorted. "I can't make a meal out of those teeny-weeny hotdogs she serves."

"Shucks," Old Sam told them, "when I was a boy, all we could afford was hotdogs and hamburgers. Everybody eats high on the hog these days. Least they eat expensive. Somehow, it don't taste the same."

Phoebe said, "Well, we'll be eating lower on the hog for awhile. I'll have to start doing some of my own baking."

Chapter Three

When Scotty McDonald returned from the ladies' powder-room, where she had left her coat, Weigand Patrick's eyes bugged. She ignored his stare.

He hissed, "One of your tits is out."

"Mind your language," she murmured. "It's the latest style. The Agnes Sorel revival."

"The *who?*"

"Agnes Sorel, the mistress of Charles the Seventh."

"Never heard of her. But if she ran around like that——"

"She was one of the most beautiful women in history."

Weigand darted his eyes around. "None of the other women have a tit showing."

She couldn't have cared less. "It's the latest thing in Paris. The Gaulle has banned it, or tried to. Not even the hereditary president of Common Europe can ban a new style."

"Holy smokes, you better not show up at the office in that get-up. The Sachem would bite the tip of it off as you walked by."

Scotty snorted her scorn. "I had all that out with him back when he was governor. He'll never lay a hand on me again. But the fashion doesn't apply to day wear. It's formal."

"Formal!" Weigand muttered. "Well, come on. Let's go and snag a drink. I've got a suspicion that you're going to wow 'em tonight. The men, at least. Stay out of the ladies' room. They'll lynch you. I wonder if Nick Stanislov has got a load on yet. The quicker he gets potted and I get him around to the Moon colonies, the quicker we can ditch this party and get over to my apartment." He leered at her.

"Huh," she said. "I haven't been to an embassy party for months. There's no hurry to get to your place."

"That's what you think."

An Italian appropriated Scotty for a dance before she'd had a chance to knock back even one of the Stolichnaya vodkas that were being passed around in wholesale lots by a full platoon of servants.

Patrick looked after her. He muttered to himself, "I'm going to have to watch that Wop. I've got her all keyed up to the sticking point. But I want to be sure *I* do the sticking."

Somebody said, "I beg your pardon? Ah, Mr. Patrick."

Weigand Patrick turned. It was young Frol Krasnaya, one of the *Pravda* men. Weigand said unhappily, "Hi, Frol. Nice turnout."

The Russian journalist was looking after Scotty and the Italian attache. "Quite a dress," he said, blinking.

Weigand Patrick tore his own eyes from the pair. He didn't like the way the Italian was jiggling. It didn't look as though it was called for in the type of dance they were doing. A waiter went by. Weigand put out a hand and grabbed a drink.

Frol Krasnaya made a half gesture with his own glass. "To Peace, Mr. Patrick. I am sorry the President couldn't make it."

Weigand grunted. "If the President came to a Russian May Day celebration, he'd lose a million votes. You have to remember, you people are still our prime bogy-men."

The other smiled regretfully. "And you are ours. I suppose every nation must have a bogy-man. It keeps the people from thinking about their real troubles."

Weigand looked at him. "You've been reading Machiavelli, Frol."

The young Russian newspaperman chuckled. "The Romans had the axiom long before Machiavelli was ever born. When you fear trouble at home, stir up war abroad."

Weigand took down half of his water-clear drink, then looked into the glass accusingly. "Holy smokes," he complained. "Haven't you got something to mix with this liquid H-bomb?"

Frol Krasnaya said, "We Russians have a few axioms of our own. One is that the only thing that mixes with vodka is more vodka."

25

The American press secretary grunted at that. "Listen, Frol," he said, as though only half interested. "What's the latest scoop on the Moon colony?"

"Moon colony?" the other said warily.

"Ummmm. I heard somewhere that you were going to increase your personnel at the moon base."

"Ah, you did? How numerous is your own group of scientists—if that is what they are—on Luna, Mr. Patrick?"

"Search me," Patrick said. He should have known better than to try to get anything out of Krasnaya. The *Pravda* man was young but not particularly stupid. However, he was anxious to get out of here. Scotty's half-bared chest wasn't conducive to allowing him to forget the original manner in which he had planned to spend the evening. And the sooner he got away from this party. . . .

He said to Krasnaya, "Where's the Ambassador? We got here a bit late. I haven't seen him yet."

"Comrade Stanislov is over there in the library with some of the, ah, more prominent guests."

Weigand Patrick looked at him.

Krasnaya said hurriedly, "Of course, he would wish the President's press secretary to join him."

"See you later, Frol," Patrick said. He shot one last agonized look in the direction of Scotty, and headed for the library. Scotty had been appropriated by a Rumanian. A Rumanian in military uniform, his waist so pinched that he must certainly have been wearing a corset. He was kind of jiggling too. Weigand wondered vaguely if it was a new dance step, or simply Scotty.

There were a round dozen guests with Nicolas Stanislov, most of them of ambassador or consul rank. As he approached, Weigand wondered what they were discussing so animatedly. The President's police action in the Antarctic? The liberation of Mozambique? Perhaps,

26

hopefully, the Moon colonies. If he could just get the Russian on that. . . .

He came up and most of those present nodded at him and some murmured his name, but Stanislov, who was speaking, wasn't interrupted. They all hung on his words.

He was saying, "This worker was employed in a pickle factory in Kiev. He had worked there for a good many years and finally he confessed to his wife that he had acquired a compulsion, a sort of, ah, neurosis. No? The fact was, he was fascinated by the idea of sticking it into the pickle slicer. He got to the point of thinking about it night and day. Finally, one day, he came home pale, obviously upset. His wife asked him what had happened and he told her the Comrade factory manager had fired him. 'Why?' she demanded. He said, 'Well, you know, all these years I've had this compulsion to stick it in the pickle slicer? Well, today I did it.' His wife stared at him, aghast. 'How are you?' she demanded. 'I'm fine,' he said. She was surprised. She said, 'Well, then, what happened to the pickle slicer?' 'Oh,' he said, 'they fired her too.'"

The assembled diplomats laughed.

A waiter went about with a fresh tray of vodka glasses. Each must have held a good three ounces, Weigand decided. He shot a look at the Russian Ambassador from the side of his eyes. Good. The man already looked slightly blurred around the edges. He'd evidently been drinking toasts since the early hours of the party.

Weigand Patrick held up his glass. "To the Moon colonies!" he toasted.

Everybody knocked back their drinks, bottoms up. Weigand followed suit and turned to Stanislov. Too late.

The Mexican Consul was saying, "Have you heard the one about Manuel and the American tourist?"

No one had heard the one about Manuel and the American tourist. The Mexican launched into the story, while Weigand groaned inwardly.

"This American tourist had a date with his wife at the fountain in the middle of the Zocalo, the town plaza. His watch had stopped and he didn't know what time it was and he was due at two o'clock. As he hurried along, he recognized Manuel stretched out prone on the grass, taking a siesta. Next to Manuel was sprawled his burro, also out like a light. The American occasionally had Manuel and his burro haul wood for the fireplace and other tasks. He stopped now and said, 'Hey, Manuel, what time is it?' Manuel opened one eye after a moment. He said, 'Senor, as you know, I am a poor man. I do not have a watch. However . . .' He reached out slowly toward the burro which was so sprawled that his scrotum projected behind him through his hind legs. Manuel took up the animal's testicles and hefted them. He said, 'It is ten minutes to two, Senor,' and closed his eyes again. The American tourist stood there for a long moment, looking at him. He hurried on toward the fountain and when he got there, he found his wife. As an afterthought, he said, 'Dear, what time do you have?' She looked at her watch and said, "Five minutes until two.' He thought about it for a minute. Finally, he said, 'Wait here. I'll be right back.' He returned to where Manuel was still sprawled and said, 'Hey, Manuel. What time is it now?' Manuel sighed, opened one eye again, reached over and hefted the burro's scrotum once more. He said, 'Senor, it is now two o'clock.' The American tourist looked at him for a long unbelieving moment. Finally, he cleared his throat and said, 'Look, I've heard about a lot of different ways of telling time. Sun dials, hourglasses, water clocks, all sorts of things. But, well, I know you Mexicans have some, well, sort of mysteries, going all the way back to the Aztecs. Things we, well, white men don't under-

28

stand. But, well, I never heard of telling time by weighing a burro's testicles. Listen, I'll give you ten pesos if you'll tell me how you do it.' Manuel opened both eyes but still didn't stir. He said, 'Senor, it is very simple. When I lift the burro's balls out of the way I can see the clock in the Cathedral.'"

All laughed.

Ambassador Stanislov stopped a passing waiter who presented a tray of vodka glasses.

Stanislov turned to Weigand and said, his glass high, "To the President of the United States of the Americas."

Everybody knocked their drinks back.

Everybody looked at Weigand Patrick.

He cleared his throat and reached for another glass. "To Andrei Zorin, Number One of the Soviet Complex!"

Everybody knocked back their drinks.

Pierre Dusage, Ambassador from Common Europe looked slightly miffed.

The Mexican Consul reached out quickly and picked up a third vodka. "To The Gaulle and Common Europe!"

Everybody knocked back their drinks.

Weigand Patrick coughed gently and began to say, "Now the Moon——"

But the Israeli cultural attache was saying, "Did you hear the one about the British oil prospector in the Arab States?"

Evidently, nobody had heard that one.

"Well," he said, "it seems that this oil prospector was driving a caravan of camels loaded down with oil-drilling equipment. He was working on a deadline and was making the best time he could across the desert. Eventually, they came to an international border between two of the small Arab States. Here they were stopped. The customs official declared it was impossible to let the male camels in the caravan through. It seemed they were very proud of their camels in this country and didn't want inferior breeds coming in and possibly crossing. The Britisher was up in the air but the Arab was adamant. Only if all the male camels were castrated would he let them past. But the Englishman argued, the nearest vet must be five hundred miles away. He couldn't possibly take the time to send for him. The Arab shrugged hugely. 'But,' he said, 'there is no need for a vet. It is very simple.' And he took up two bricks and came up behind the nearest camel and smashed the animal's testicles. The Englishman went pale and clutched his stomach. 'Oh, no,' he said. 'Oh, no. I can't bear it.' The Arab looked at him, surprised. 'What is the matter?' he said. The Englishman said, 'Oh, no. I can't bear the thought. The pain!' 'But,' the Arab said, 'there is no pain.' The Britisher stared at him. 'No pain!' The Arab shook his head and held up the two bricks. 'Only if you get your thumbs between the bricks.' "

All laughed.

A new waiter came up.

Weigand Patrick was beginning to feel the last round of toasts, but good. He looked owlishly at Nick Stanislov who was obviously also feeling no pain.

The Indian Consul said, "We have toasted the President, Number One and The Gaulle. I now propose a toast to everlasting peace between them all."

Everybody knocked back their drinks.

Ambassador Stanislov took up another hooker of vodka and held it high. "Not only peace, but cultural coexistence."

Everybody knocked their drinks back.

Everybody stared at Weigand Patrick. He could begin to feel the fog rolling in, but he took up the new glass the servant proffered.

"Uhhh," he said. "To the Moon colonies."

"We did that one," the Mexican Consul protested in a slur. "I wish this were tequila. I can drink tequila all night."

But everybody else had knocked theirs back.

Ambassador Dusage looked embarrassed. He said, "We have forgotten to toast President Cantinflas, of Mexico."

Everybody knocked that one back.

Weigand Patrick could quite distinctly feel the fog rolling in now.

However, the Russian was talking to him. From far, far away his voice said, "Ah, you are interested in the Moon colonies, Mr. Patrick?"

"Sure . . . sure am . . ." Weigand could hear his own voice from away, far away. He didn't quite seem to be in control of it, but he could hear it. "Sure am . . . Moon colo-kneed. I mean . . ."

The fog was swirling higher.

The Russian was saying. Well, he was saying something.

. . . hydroponics . . . complete self-service, self-sufficient . . . closed aquarium . . . true colony . . . glory of Soviet space . . . eliminate need for freight transport . . .

The fog rolled all the way in.

For a brief moment, the fog rolled out again, in swirls.

Weigand Patrick was in a hovercar limousine. One of the White House limousines. Scotty was driving. Her coat was back on. He was subjected not to the Agnes Sorel revival style.

He shook his head and tried to say something.

"Shut up, you drunken sot."

He was mildly indignant. "What do you mean, drunken sot? What other kind of sot is there? Besides . . . besides, I did it for my country."

31

"Great. Just what was accomplished for the U.S. and A. by passing out into the arms of the Common Europe ambassador?"

"Good ol' Pierre," Weigand slurred. "Always in the middle. Dependable in emergency. Where we going?"

"Where we started out for. Your apartment," she said bitterly. "I had to get one of the Polish attaches to help me drag you out."

"Good," he said. "Tonight's the night, eh Scotty, ol' girl. Tonight's the night."

She snorted.

And the fog rolled in again.

When the fog rolled out, partially, he was seated on the edge of his bed, in shirt sleeves, pants and socks.

Scotty was hunkered down before him, tugging at his pants legs, snorting and muttering incoherently.

"Hey," he said. "Take it easy."

"Shut up," she told him. "Ha! The great lover. Casanova, Don Juan, Errol Flynn. Ha!"

The fog rolled in again.

When the fog rolled out, it was morning. Well into the morning. He was in bed, in his own apartment. He was dressed in nothing save his undershorts.

He looked hopefully at the place next to him. But nobody was there and the pillow showed no signs of anyone having been there.

Weigand Patrick groaned pathetically.

Chapter Four

When Marv Sellers returned home after sitting around with the others at the union hall, he was surprised to find Phoebe there. He looked at his watch, then remembered that it had stopped and that he hadn't wanted to spend the money for repairs.

He opened the refrigerator door and peered in hopefully, although he was well aware that there hadn't been any beer for a week, and that he had checked to make sure he hadn't missed one last plastic every day since that sad milestone.

Marv grunted disappointment and said over his shoulder, "What the hell you doing home, Phoebe?"

Phoebe Sellers made her mouth into a bitter moue. "Fired," she said.

"Fired, for crissake!"

She said, "The company's big item here in Tucson was distributing all these gadgets like. You know, nuclear back scratchers, electric toothbrushes, automatic Martini stirrers, that sort of thing. Evidently, people finally got around to the fact they could do without them. So the company folded. Even Mr. Edwards' gone on relief."

"Oh great," Marv groaned. "Now we're both unemployed and all our payments coming up."

Phoebe tried to surface her basic optimism. She said, "Look, Marv, we can sell the car. It's only a year and a half old and nearly paid for. We'll get several thousand dollars for it."

"Oh yeah. You oughta see all the used cars on the lots."

"We won't sell it through a dealer, we'll put a ad in the paper."

He said, "What'll we do without a car? I need it to get to work . . . if I get a job."

Old Sam had come in. He chuckled, almost happily. "Gettin' to be like old times," he said. "I usta ride to work on a bike, when I was a kid. More fun than a car."

33

"Knock it, Gramps," Marv growled. "And it's no use looking in the refrigerator. There ain't no beer, and there's not gonna be no beer. Too damn expensive."

Nevertheless, Old Sam peered into the box, duplicating the hopeful expression of Marv a bit earlier. He grunted disgust and made his way over to his rocker.

"We gotta do something about that," he said. "Especially with the hot weather coming up."

Phoebe shook her head and began making preparation of a sparse evening meal. "No beer, Gamps, it just ain't in the budget."

Old Sam said thoughtfully, "In days past, my old man usta make his own beer. Had all these crocks, brewing away. Way I remember back to it, he usta figure it cost him something like two anna half cents to make a quart." Sam chuckled. "Sometimes he made the stuff too strong or somethin' and it blew the bottles up."

Marv looked at him. "That's the trouble," he said. "You'd hafta buy bottles and all." But there was a thoughtful element in his voice.

Sam said, "I saw a whole lotta bottles over near to the city dump. They don't use 'em much nowadays. When I was a boy we got everything in bottles. Milk, beer, everything. All these plastics and crap like that came later."

"I'll bet," Marv said.

Old Sam said, "Heh, heh, lot of things to remind you of the old days."

"Listen, what else d'you need besides bottles?"

Bill Waters flicked off his phone screen and muttered "Balls."

Miss Harding flinched only slightly. "I beg your pardon, Mr. Waters?" Actually, she was by now long familiar with the expletive.

"Balls," he snorted. "Balls. You've heard the old saying, *Balls, said the queen, if I had them I'd be king.*"

Miss Harding was taken aback. She said, "Yes, sir."

"That was old man Benington cancelling the only order we've had for over a month. And I figured that was the one sure sale coming up. He's the only man left in town with enough money in his sock to buy anything more expensive than a used fart."

She ignored the latter part of that and looked distressed. "Why, that's terrible, Mr. Waters. He was just here the other day and was so definite about needing a car."

Waters growled, "He bought a used car from some damn bricklayer who sold it for less than half price. How can I compete with that sort of thing?"

"I don't know, Mr. Waters. I . . . I heard the new models aren't going to have any chrome at all. Bring down the price. Possibly that will be an inducement."

"That's right," he grunted in disgust. "So there's a crisis in the chrome industry. They've laid off something like five thousand men. Which means exactly five thousand families more not in the market for cars this year. And everything's air-cushion hovercars this year. No tires. You know what that's done to the rubber industry up in Akron?"

"No sir."

"Well, use your imagination."

He came to his feet, prowled over to the watercooler and located the sole remaining paper cup they had been using the past several days.

He drew himself a drink, knocked it back stiff-wristed, as though it was gin, and drew another. The bottom dropped out of the cup, at long last soaked through, and the water dumped into the wastebasket below. He stood there for a long, suffering minute.

Miss Harding said brightly, "By the way, Mr. Waters. We seem to be out of typewriter ribbons. I need one for my machine."

He snorted deprecation of that remark. "Fine. But even if I had the money for such items as typewriter ribbons, I don't know where you'd buy any. Did you know Keefer's stationery store just folded up? Who needs stationery these days? There's so little business correspondence, I'm surprised the post office doesn't call it a day."

Miss Harding said, "There're other stationery stores, further downtown, sir." She thought about it for a moment before adding cautiously, "I think."

He came to a sudden decision. "Well, that cancellation is the straw that broke this ruptured camel's back. Notify the men out in the shop that I'm closing."

She looked both distressed and sympathetic. "The usual two weeks severance pay, Mr. Waters?"

He laughed bitterly. "Where do you think I'd get it, Miss Harding? My father-in-law's offered me a job as delivery boy for his delicatessen. He's fired the two he used to have. Wants to keep the job in the family."

Chapter Five

Weigand Patrick ambled into the office of the President's personal secretary, the inevitable corncob, which was his own pet affectation and distinctive mark invariably used by the political cartoonists, slung from the side of his mouth.

Scotty didn't look up, but she said, "How did the

press conference go? Did Old Chucklehead wow them?"

Weigand said, "There wasn't any. Fred and I tried to brief him but he was afraid to face the music. I went over to the press lobby and told them the President couldn't be present because he had a headache and Samuelson from the *Times* said he didn't doubt it, and Harrison from *Newsweek* said no wonder."

"So then?"

"So then I offered to answer any questions and they looked at me for awhile and finally they began telling limericks."

"Limericks?"

"Listen to this one. Simak, from the *Guardian*."

"There once was a man named Durkin,
"Who was always jerkin' his gerkin.
    "Said his wife, one day,
    "Deprived of her lay,
"Durkin, you're shirkin' yer ferkin' by jerkin' your
        gerkin, you bastard."

Scotty looked at him. "That doesn't scan, and besides, it doesn't even rhyme. Bastard doesn't rhyme with Durkin."

"A critic," he protested, fishing matches from his pocket.

Polly Adams wandered in vaguely and said, "Hello, Weigand, hello Miss McDonald. You haven't seen Hilda, have you?"

Weigand Patrick slouched to his feet, from where he had been perched on the side of Scotty's desk, and took his pipe from his mouth.

"Good afternoon, Mrs. Adams," he said.

Polly Adams said archly, "Oh, do call me Polly, Weigand. After all these years."

Scotty said, "I haven't seen your Social Secretary for

days, Mrs. Adams. The last time was during the reception for the Congolese Ambassador. She was, uh, rather fed up with all the poison pen letters."

Polly Adams looked about the office, as though in faint hope. "I'm surprised you don't have a bit of a bar in here, Miss MacDonald. Such an important little office, the President's personal secretary."

Scotty said, "Mrs. Adams, if I had a bit of a bar in here, half the people that got in to see Old Chuckle . . . , that is, the President, would be smashed. Half the people that go through this office, are still nervous about meeting the President. Well, nearly half these days."

The butler entered through the door the First Lady had used only moments before and stood politely.

Weigand said, "Hello, William."

Polly Adams turned to the newcomer. "What is it, William?"

The butler announced, "Madam, the ladies of the Potted Planters Gardening Society are here."

"The who?"

"The Potted Planters."

"Already, at this time of the day?"

"Yes, Madam. Should I see about tea for them?"

"Tea?" Polly said vaguely. "Do they look like the types that blast? No, no William, you're apt to overdo. I suggest from your description of the state they're already in, that you serve Planter's Punches. Ummm, and William . . ."

"Yes, Madam?"

"Put a stick in them."

"Yes, Madam."

William, his aplomb visibly shaken, about faced and more or less staggered out.

The First Lady, somewhat brightened, said, "Oh, dear, another society to greet. However, it's so important for Horace. I suppose I'll have to entertain them."

When she was gone, Scotty and Weigand looked after her emptily.

Scotty said, "Why didn't you say something?"

"What? But that reminds me. The boys have been writing some snide remarks about Polly listing to starboard, almost everytime she shows up in public. I'll have to plant the story that she's got a pierced ear drum. Throws off her sense of balance."

Scotty snorted and got up and went over to one of the businesslike files that lined one wall of the tiny office.

Weigand blurted, "Holy smokes, what's happened to your clothes?"

She smirked at him over her shoulder. "You like this outfit?"

"Like it? Where is it?"

"Don't be prehistoric. It's the latest thing from Common Europe. London. They call it the Minuskirt."

"Minus skirt? You mean you're going around like that on purpose?"

"Of course, silly." She started back for her desk, a folder in hand. "You can't see anything that you can't see on any beach."

"I can see anything, on any beach, what with these new bottomless bathing suits. What's that got to do with it?"

She sniffed contempt of his opinions. "Besides, I can tell you like it by the expression of your pants."

"Keep your obscene cracks to yourself, Scotty Mac Donald. However, I'm glad to see you're a red head all over."

39

"Now who's making obscene cracks?" She looked down, doubtfully. "Besides, you're a liar. They aren't *that* transparent."

"Listen," Weigand Patrick said earnestly, "that brings something to mind. When are we going to do that bed scene?"

"What do you mean it *brings* something to mind? When was your mind ever clear on the subject?"

"Well, I'll tell you one thing, it's not going to be as long as you run around in outfits like that. No wonder the textile industry is in the biggest slump in history. How in the hell can they sell any women's clothing when you broads are reunning around without skirts and with bottomless bathing suits?"

Scotty decided to ignore him. She looked at the schedule on the desk top. "Isn't Old Chucklehead expecting you?"

"Look, you oughten to call the Sachem that. He's the President of the United States of the Americas."

"Yes, and I'm his personal secretary and have been for years and if there's anybody who knows what to call him, it's me."

"All right, all right." Weigand Patrick began heading for the door to the presidential office. "However, let's get together on that big defloweration scene."

"Ha!" she snorted after him. "After what happened the last time?"

"I can explain that."

"You can explain anything, you demi-buttocked Casanova."

The oval study on the second floor of the White House was empty. Weigand Patrick looked around in mild surprise and fished in his jacket for his pipe. He wondered if his ultimate superior had snuck out the back way again, in that silly disguise of his, to get smashed and play poker with some of the lobbyists and hangers-on who had taken up residence in Greater Washington when Horace Adams graduated from governor of his state to Chief Executive. The Secret Service boys had one hell of a hassle finding him the last time.

However, at that moment Weigand Patrick spotted a figure standing alone on the second-story back porch. He pushed open the glass door and stepped out onto the cool and sunlit erpanse and joined the other.

"Chief," he said.

The President turned. His handsome face was unhappy, and obviously in thought, which was as ever in itself of passing surprise to his press secretary-cum-special-assistant.

Horace Adams said, "Son, Jimmy just reported on the latest polls. Did you know my popularity rating, my public image, has sunk to a new low?"

Weigand Patrick said, "I didn't know what was possible, Mr. President. I thought it was already as low as it could get."

"They've got a new system, evidently," the President muttered lowly. "For the first time in history, a president's popularity is being rated in negative percentages."

"Negative percentages?" Weigand said, scratching a match and lighting the corncob.

Horace Adams was disgusted. "Evidently, in the old days the polls would indicate that, say, 55% of the public approved the way you were handling the administration. If you were lucky, it might get up to 75% or if things were going bad, it might drop to as low as 35% during something like the Bay of Pigs, or the U-2 overflight, or the Asian War. But this is the first time we've had a negative number from a poll."

Weigand Patrick closed his eyes in pain.

41

The President said accusingly, "What in the name of Moses do you smoke in that thing, shredded army blanket?"

Weigand put his pipe in his jacket pocket and followed his superior back into the presidential study.

Horace Adams took his place behind his desk. His eyes went down to his feet and he snorted. "You'd think after all these years, you wouldn't be able to see those holes from the golf shoes. I wish I played golf. Anything to get out of here. Have you ever seen the statistics on the amount of time Ike played golf while he was holding down this job?"

"No," Patrick told him. "And you don't really want to get out of here, Sir. Which brings up the matter of the next election. We're going to have to start thinking about that."

"I have been thinking about it. Smogborne thinks we ought to call a moratorium on it."

Weigand winced. "A moratorium?"

"Because of the emergency. The country's in an emergency. Call off the election, until it's over."

Weigand leaned forward. "Look, Chief. The country's been in an emergency since Roosevelt. He was the first president to come up with the advantages of an emergency. This, that and the other thing had to be postponed until the emergency was over. Special taxes were levied to help take care of it. Evidently, the emergency never ended, certainly the taxes never did. If it wasn't a depression it was a new war, either cold or hot, or a missile lag, or the red-threat, or whatever. By this time, the Chief Executive has taken over every power Congress used to have, except kissing babies. But this is a new one, declaring a moratorium on the next presidential election."

The presidential expression amounted to just short of

a pout. "Well, what's the difference?" he grumbled. "Craminently, Son, you know very well there hasn't been any difference between the Republicans and the Democrats for the past ten elections or so. Why go through the routine of pretending there is and holding a campaign?"

"Well, Chief, the public likes to have the optical illusion dangled there before their eyes. Periodically, they like to take one figurehead out and put a new one in. They don't particularly care, evidently, whether the new one is any different. They just like a change."

"Well, let them change something else. I've got the Far-Out Society to worry about."

A small light flickered on the desk and Horace Adams scowled at it and said, "Yes?"

His Appointment Secretary's voice said, "Mr. President, you are scheduled for the meeting with the brain trust."

"Oh, yes, of course. Thank you, Fred." He came to his feet. "Let's go, Son."

Weigand Patrick followed him through the outer office, where Fred Moriarty dropped in behind the procession, and down the hall to the Cabinet Room.

The others were already there, seated about the horseshoe-like Cabinet table. The President muttered some sort of a greeting, when they came to their feet, and took his place at the head. Weigand Patrick sat immediately behind him to his left, and Fred Moriarty behind him to his right. The professors, economists, sociologists and psychologists sat about in a circle, dimly reminiscent of King Arthur and his Round Table.

The President had on his Tri-Di personality—to begin with. He said brightly, "All right, uh, . . . you."

Weigand Patrick leaned forward and whispered, "Leland Markham, Harvard, economist, recently published *The New Unaffluent Society.*"

43

"Yes, yes," Horace Adams muttered, and aloud, "Your report, Professor Markup?"

Patrick whispered, "Markham," but was ignored.

Professor Markham shuffled his papers in full stereotype. He said, a hurt quality in his voice, "Our road-building program didn't exactly turn out the way we thought, Mr. President."

The President scowled. "Why not? It was a natural. Put men to work all over the country building the roads, mining the needed materials, asphalt, cement, everything. You had it all worked out. Very impressive charts. Computer reports, everything."

The professor cleared his throat apologetically. "Yes, sir. It was all right as long as we were *building* the roads on a crash basis. It is what happened afterwards we didn't anticipate." He cleared his throat again. "The fact is, these newer, wider roads enabled the truck companies to move freight faster and hence with fewer men and trucks. Since the roads are so straight and strong, it also enabled them to use larger trucks. Now fewer drivers are needed, and since there are fewer trucks, less mechanics. Besides that, the competition had crowded out various railroads and resulted in the remaining cutting down their daily freight car loadings. The long term result has been greater unemployment."

The President groaned softly. "I'll never end this confounded depression and get my Far-Out Society underway," he complained. He turned to the next intellectual looking type.

Patrick leaned forward, "Doctor Smyth. Winchester Smyth, physicist and engineer. Stanford. The dam project. New water for irrigation, new hydro-electric . . ."

"Oh, yes, yes," the President muttered. He turned to the other, "Well, Doctor?"

44

The other expressed discomfort. "I am afraid my report has similarities to Professor Markham's."

The President turned off what remained of his Tri-Di personality and said coldly, "You were pretty happy about it as I recall."

"Well, yes, Mr. President. As a temporary make-work project, building the dam employed tens of thousands of men, and even a good many women office workers."

"What could possibly go wrong?"

"Well, when the dams were completed, they opened up wide areas of former desert to agriculture. As you know, given water, desert areas can prove fabulously fertile. Also, these areas were so flat they particularly lent themselves to automated farming." The doctor shook his head mournfully. "There's been a double result. We're producing more surplus farm products than ever, but at the same time the smaller farmers are being driven to the wall because they can't compete."

The President closed his eyes for a moment, in pain. He muttered accusingly, "Why couldn't we have built the dams where there wasn't any water?"

When there was no immediate response to that he said, "Anything else?"

"Well, yes, Mr. President. There was another side effect. The new dams, with the very latest hydroelectric generating equipment have released so much additional power that several projected nuclear power plants in those areas have been cancelled. At this stage they couldn't compete with water power. It has . . ." he hesitated before breaking the news ". . . led to the dismissal of several thousands of construction and nuclear power workers."

"Craminently," the President complained. He thought about it for awhile, causing all to drop into a surprised silence. Finally he said, "We could sabotage the new dams. Blow them up some dark night." He looked at his appointment secretary. "Fred, what department of government would that come under?"

Fred Moriarty said apologetically, "Mr. President, I don't think there is a department devoted to blowing up government projects. We would have to form one."

Horace Adams glared around the table. "Does anybody have any *good* news?"

Somebody rustled papers and said meekly, "I have a report here that the Bull Durham Company is booming."

"Bill Durham?" the President said.

Weigand Patrick leaned forward. "A roll-your-own cigarette company, Chief. The, ah, tailor-made cigarette companies aren't doing so good. Neither are liquor companies, and the breweries. With taxes so high, and pay falling off so fast, everybody's making bathtub gin and homebrew."

One cheerful faced type chirped, "Well, here's one from the plus side of the ledger, Mr. President. We've finally got every men jack of the military forces back home, and most of them out of uniform. Had a bit of trouble in some of the special officer clubs, PX stores, and officer housing communities, in such countries as Germany and Spain. They threw up barricades. Had to send in the paratroopers to root them out, but it's all finished now. It will cut literally billions from our expenditures and free the money to use to fight the depression."

"Money, we can use," somebody muttered. "Some of our plans, originally evolved to solve world problems at bargain basement prices, are running into financial escalation. Project Porpoise, for instance. We thought

46

that once we got the herds of whales going, the cost would be minimal."

The President glared at the speaker. "What's wrong with Project Porpoise? That's one of my favorite Far-Out Society operations. Feed all the underdeveloped countries with whale meat."

The other cleared his throat, apologetically. "It seems, Mr. President, that the porpoises are demanding full pay. The same pay the average cowboy gets in Texas."

"What! Those damn wetbacks!"

Fred Moriarty said, "There's a side development to this cutting down on the army, Mr. President."

Everybody looked at him. He said, unhappily. "The veterans. They're forming organizations. One is demanding free tickets on the airlines. First class tickets, with meals, to march on Greater Washington so they can demand a bonus."

A feisty, bearded type from across the table snapped, "There is one matter I think must come to your attention, Mr. President. When we raised tariffs so that foreign commodities wouldn't flood our remaining domestic markets, we put Common Europe and the rest of the world into a tizzy. They raised tariffs right back at us, and our exports have fallen to the vanishing point."

"Well, then at least it balances off even," the President grumbled.

"Not exactly, Mr. President. You see, our economy depends upon the import of copper from Chile, oil and iron ore from Venezuela, tin from Bolivia, and so forth. As a result, we've been spending money abroad consistently, but not making any by exports. Our gold is flowing away from Fort Knox as though there were a leak in the vaults." The feisty one ventured a sour laugh.

Nobody joined him.

Fred Moriarty said, "Mr. President, I think, while we're on the subject of Common Europe and other foreign countries, I ought to bring your attention to another aspect of the withdrawing of our troops from abroad. It seems that it's caused a full scale depression, not only in Common Europe but Japan, Siam—all the countries where we used to have bases. Hundreds of thousands of pimps, whores, bartenders, B-Girls, strip-teasers, hostesses —not to speak of pickpockets, touts, black-marketeers, and types specializing in such endeavor as rolling drunks—have been thrown out of work. All these people were big spenders. When their incomes dried up, business collapsed abroad."

The President looked over his shoulder at Weigand Patrick and muttered, "So this is a brain trust."

Weigand Patrick shrugged apologetically.

Horace Adams again faced the assembly. "Well, where do we go from here, gentlemen? The first time we met, everybody had a pet scheme."

One military-looking type, though dressed now in mufti, cleared his throat.

Patrick leaned forward and murmured, "Major General Oscar Fallout, Retired. The brain trust's military advisor. Before this job, he worked as an advisor for the Napalm, Bazooka and Thumbscrews Manufacturing Company and before that in procurement in the Octagon."

The President said, "Well, general?"

"Yes, sir. I have had passed on to me from a special committee representing the munitions industry, a suggestion that seems fraught with interesting possibilities."

"Well, go on, go on . . ."

"Mr. President, in the past, possible depressions were headed off by military expenditures. Korea came along just in time to give a spurt to lagging heavy industry.

When that scrap unfortunately came to an end, we had the Asian War."

One of the economists snapped, "If you are suggesting another war, general, we might point out to you that they aren't exactly practical any more."

"No, no, not that. I realize, as do all senior military men, that with nuclear weapons, wars can no longer be called upon to solve economic problems, desirable as they used to be. In the past, generals were able to sit comfortably twenty or more miles to the rear and order the lads to take such and such a hill, fort, or whatever, at all costs. But now, when the bombs drop, even generals get killed." The last came out with a certain degree of indignation.

"So," the President said, intrigued, "what is it that this special committee of the munitions industry has come up with?"

"Well, Mr. President, the committee is of the opinion that present laws pertaining to homicide are too, ah, stringent."

Horace Adams blinked. "Stringent?"

General Fallout was shaking his head. "Much too stringent. The committee suggests that each citizen be allowed two homicides. The solving of the population explosion would be a side effect, but most beneficial. But the boom in pistols, rifles, submachine guns, armored vests, ammunition, and so forth, would put the country's industry back into high gear." The general's eyes were flashing inspiration.

Weigand Patrick said gently, "General Fallout, I am afraid you are a dreamer before your time."

But the President was looking thoughtfully at his right-hand man. "I don't know, son. Let's not be too hasty about this." He tapped the side of his nose with a forefinger.

Weigand dropped his voice to a murmur, "Chief, if every citizen of the United States of the Americas was allowed two homicides, or even one, do you think you'd live the week out?"

The President coughed then said, "I am afraid your scheme is impractical, general. Does anyone else have anything to offer?"

A finger rose to request attention.

Patrick murmured, "Dr. Warren Dempsey Witherson, of Moppett, Hastings and Witherson. Public relations. Handled your last campaign."

"Of course, of course." The President beamed down the table at Witherson. "Yes, Doctor?"

Warren Dempsey Witherson came to his feet, his pince-nez glasses in his right hand, an aura of dignity about him.

He said, "Mr. President, I suggest a think tank of businessmen."

"Think tank?" the President said blankly.

Weigand leaned forward, "Chief, Roosevelt had his Brain Trust, Kennedy had his Irish Mafia, Truman had his whiz-kids, and Johnson had his think tanks. Groups of ultra intelligent scientists, philosophers and so forth who'd sit around together and think problems out to a conclusion. Interaction of ideas, that sort of thing."

The President looked over at Fred Moriarty indignantly. "Why doesn't anybody ever tell me anything around here?" He turned back to Warren Dempsey Witherson and his Tri-Di personality was on him again. In fact, he beamed.

"A think tank of businessmen to come up with some way of getting us out of the depression. Tell me more, Doctor. . . ."

Chapter Six

Warren Dempsey Witherson's copter-cab flitted in to the landing ramp of the Doolittle Building and came to a gentle halt.

Witherson peered about, holding his pince-nez glasses to the upper bridge of his nose with the forefinger of his left hand. There was no one else on the ramp for the moment. He cleared his throat and tried the door of the auto-taxi. It, as usual though not always, Witherson had long since found, didn't budge.

He looked at the auto-meter and the sign beneath it which read, *The Slot Will Take Bills or Coins of Any Denomination and Return Your Correct Change.*

Warren Dempsey Witherson peered nervously to right and left again, dipped his thumb and first two fingers into a vest pocket and came forth with a dollar-sized iron slug. He dropped it into the auto-meter slot and waited for his twenty cents change before opening the door and stepping out.

He set his conservatively cut coat, jiggled his malacca cane in preliminary to getting under way, and headed for the building's entrance.

The Doolittle Building was ostentatiously swank and boasted a live receptionist.

Warren Dempsey Witherson bent a kindly eye upon her and fished about in his pockets absently until he came up with a business card. He pushed his glasses back and blinked at the card as though wondering where he had seen the like before. However, he handed it over.

Miss Evans was crisp, after inspecting it. "Yes, Doctor Witherson. Whom was it you wished to see?"

51

"Eh? Of course, my dear. Professor Doolittle."

Only the slightest flicker indicated she was taken aback. "You have an appointment, Doctor? Perhaps one of his secretaries . . ."

"Appointment? An appointment? Certainly not, my dear." Doctor Witherson beamed at her forgivingly.

Miss Evans placed the card on a scanner and said something softly into an efficient-looking gadget which sat, small and inconspicuous, to her right.

There was a slight flicker again just before she said, "Professor Doolittle will see you immediately, Doctor. He is sending one of his secretaries down."

"Of course, my dear."

The secretary hurried from the lift and came trotting forward. "Doctor Witherson? So sorry to have kept you waiting. Professor Doolittle sent me. I'm Walthers, Doctor."

"Fine, my boy," Witherson beamed at him.

The lift, unlike the others serving the building, was unlettered and Walthers used a key to open its door. It bore them to the highest reaches of the edifice in the shortest of order.

Professor Doolittle came to his feet immediately and marched forward, a heavy paw outstretched, when the two entered his office, which involved the better part of a quarter acre of floor space.

"That will be all, Walthers," he said. "And be sure I am undisturbed, no matter the circumstance." Professor Doolittle puffed out apple red cheeks to the point of resembling Santa Claus.

"Yes, sir." Walthers was gone.

The two men stood back from each other and grinned inanely.

"The Funked-Out Kid!"

"The Professor!"

"By George, it's been a long time, Kid."

"Since . . . let's see, Tangier. Last mark we copped a score from was that winchell in Tangier."

"The last I heard of you, Kid, somebody told me you failed to properly cool off a mark you had just taken on a Big Con down in Miami." The Professor turned and headed for an impressive, volume-heavy bookcase, which turned out to be an imperial-size bar upon the flicking of a hand over an eye-button.

The Funked-Out Kid followed him. "The fix had curdled and for a while I was warm, but I wasn't sneezed."

The Professor chuckled, "What will it be, Kid? You used to drink rye."

The drinks in hand, they found chairs and grinned at each other some more.

Both were in their sixties, but there resemblance ended. Mutt and Jeff came to mind, or perhaps the comedians of yesteryear, Abbott and Costello. The Funked-Out Kid was thin and nervous, The Professor, short, bulky and jovial.

The Professor looked down at the Funked-Out Kid's business card which the receptionist had sent up to him via Walthers. He cackled amusement. "You know, Kid, I almost had them send you packing. Then the name came back to me. Warren Dempsey Witherson. That is an imposing moniker for a grifter." He read from the card. "Ph.D., D.D., LL.D., Litt. D. That is rather laying it on thick, by George."

The Kid adjusted his pince-nez in dignity. "They're all the McCoy, Professor. I bought those doctorates from some of the top diploma mills in Tennessee."

The Professor, chuckling still, made them fresh drinks, returned to his chair, shot a quick glance at his watch. "Well, Kid, it is a real pleasure to see you again. If you are in town for awhile, we ought to get together some night for some reminiscences. Phone up a couple of curves, get a bit intoxicated, that sort of thing. Meanwhile, ah, how is the taw, Kid?"

The Funked-Out Kit scowled at him, then of a sudden broke into a whinny of humor which grew in volume.

It was the Professor's turn to scowl. "Confound it, what is the matter, Kid?"

The Kid let it run down and pushed his glasses back to the high bridge of his nose with his left forefinger. He shook his head. "That's a laugh," he said. "How's the taw? Professor, did you think I came up here to shake you down for a score?"

"I would not put it that way, Kid. We're old timers, By George. Comrades in arms. If your taw is in bad shape . . ." His attitude touched on the pompous.

The Kid grinned at him. "I'm here on business, Professor. What'd you think I've been doing these past fifteen years?"

"I would not know. But once a grifter, always a grifter, Kid."

Warren Dempsey Witherson let his eyes go about the overly swank office. "That doesn't seem to apply to you, Professor."

"Like Hades it doesn't, By George. Kid, I am at the top of the heap in the biggest con since some prehistoric grifter dreamed up religion and put ninety-five percent of the human race on the sucker list. Motivational Research the double-domes call it. Why, Kid, there is not a perfume house in New York that would okay the pornography of their latest ad campaign without checking it out with my lads."

"I know," the Kid said, crossing thin legs. "That's why I'm here, Professor."

The Professor looked at him. "By George," he said. "You do look prosperous at that, Kid. Like you used to in the old days, just after copping a 'sizeable score. What is your line now, the wire, the rag, the pay-off? Do you use a Big Store?"

The Funked-Out Kid was whinnying again. "We call it public relations, Professor."

"Public relations! Kid, I just cannot see you, particularly in that Ph.D. get-up you are affecting, running around trying to get columnists to plug some Tri-Di starlet just because you have gotten her to wear one of those bottomless swim suits."

"Professor, I'm not getting through to you. Haven't you ever heard of Moppett, Hastings and Witherson, the top PR outfit on the coast? No conning columnists for this grifter. I deal only with top strategy, over-all policy on the highest levels."

"That means, one assumes, you get somebody else to do the work."

`"Of course. I tell you, in this field you couldn't knock the marks if you tried."

The Professor brought the bottle of ancient Maryland rye from the bar and set it on the coffee table between them.

"Kid, I fail to see where motivational research, interviews in depth, the applying of psychoanalytical techniques to market investigation and the various other jazz we deal with, could tie in with public relations."

Warren Dempsey Witherson leaned forward to launch his pitch. "It's a big operation, Professor. My PR outfit and your motivational research agency are just two elements. Also involved are a Tri-Di studio, a couple of ad agencies, a couple of toy manufacturers, a TV network and a few more of the boys."

The Professor looked at him. "Big operation is correct."

"To make it brief, Professor, we're going to manufacture a fad. Remember, back when we were youngsters, the Davy Crockett fad? Started off as a movie. Before it was through there were being sold more than 300 Davy Crockett products."

"I remember, By George. Coonskin hats, buckskin shirts, flintlock rifles, Davy Crockett records."

"Right," the Funked-Out Kid beamed in satisfaction. "In all, it was estimated that a third of a billion dollars was spent on that fad."

The Professor hissed through his dentures.

"And they were amateurs," the Kid said. "They exploited it hit and miss. Fell into some of the best scores by pure accident. This time, Professor, we're going to milk our fad like pros." He took off his pince-nez glasses and shook them at the other.

"We got a new angle, Professor. Most of these fads are aimed at kids. Davy Crockett, the hula hoop, the Space Man fad. But kids don't have money to spend. Not the way grown up marks do. So this fad is going to be for adults."

"Go on," the Professor said. "Confound it, you've got me interested."

"That's all," Warren Dempsey Witherson beamed. "We're all set to go. We're going to settle on an adult hero, make a movie, write some songs, manufacture a fad like never before, and we're going to milk it all ways from Tuesday. The winchells won't know what hit them. And best of all, it's all legit."

"You mean the fix is in? By George, Kid, an operation of this magnitude would be nationwide. How could you possible manage it?"

Witherson continued to beam. "Professor, the fix goes all the way to the White House. As a matter of fact, I am part of President Adams' brain trust. As such, I suggested a think tank of businessmen, which intrigued him.

It has been formed. The Opedipus Group, we call ourselves."

"Oedipus Group?"

"It's Greek. Very impressive."

"You don't mean *Eidos*, do you Kid?"

"What does that mean?" Witherson scowled.

"Eidos, from the Greek *eidos*, something seen, form, akin to. Actually, the formal contents of a culture, encompassing its system of ideas, criteria for interpreting experience, and so forth."

Warren Dempsey Witherson was shaking his head in admiration. "I can see, Professor we've got to have you in the think tank."

The Professor leaned back. "By George, the whole thing is rather inspiring the way you propose it, Kid. Just who have you decided upon to feature as this adult hero?"

"We don't know."

The Professor looked at him.

"That's where you come in, Professor," the Funked-Out Kid said reasonably.

Chapter Seven

The knock at the door came in the middle of the night, as Frol Krasnaya had always thought it would. He had been but four years of age when the knock had come that first time and the three large men had given his father a matter of only minutes to dress and accompany them. He could barely remember his father.

The days of the police state were over, in the Soviet

Complex, so they told you. The cult of personality was a thing of the past. The long series of five-year plans and seven-year plans were over and all goals had been achieved. The new constitution guaranteed personal liberties. No longer were you subject to police brutality at the merest whim. So they told you.

But fears die hard, particularly when they are largely of the subconscious. And he had always, deep within, expected the knock. However, not here in Greater Washington, even in the grounds of the spacious Soviet Complex Embassy where Frol Krasnaya, in common with all other Soviet personnel, were quartered.

Frol Krasnaya allowed himself but one chill of apprehension, then rolled from his bed, squared slightly stooped shoulders, and made his way to the door. He flicked on the light and opened up, even as the burly, empty-faced zombi there was preparing to pound again.

The first of the zombi twins said expressionlessly, "Comrade Frol Krasnaya?"

If tremor there was in his voice, it was negligible. He said, "That is correct. Uh . . . to what do I owe this intrusion upon my privacy?" The last in the way of bravado.

The other ignored the question. "Get dressed and come with us, Comrade."

At least, they still called him comrade, that was something.

The zombis stood watching him emptily as he dressed.

They marched him down to the mansion lawn where a mini-jet helicopter awaited them. At this time of night, the grounds were deserted. They swooped into the air, and in ten minutes were at the Johnson Memorial International Jet Port.

When they disembarked from the small craft, the two goons assumed positions to each side of him, and they began to march toward a long, low Tupolev rocket-jet. He considered only briefly shouting and running for it. Defecting to the West. The trouble was, the West wasn't particularly interested in defectors from the Soviet Complex any more. There had been so many of them, over the years, that they were a drug on the market. And with all the unemployment these days, jobs for Soviet citizens on the lam were hard to come by.

Inside the craft, he was moderately surprised. He, and his two zombis, were evidently the sole passengers, and it was outfitted in luxury, greater luxury than he had ever run into in an aircraft before. In fact, he was dubious that even Ambassador Nicolas Stanislov would have ordinarily so traveled.

There was no mystery as to their destination. The jets whooshed them into the upper reaches, and then the rockets took over. They were landing at the Vnokovo airport within two hours, a two hours that had been spent without communication with the two police goons. A monstrously large Zim hover limousine was awaiting them to speed them into Moscow.

They by-passed Red Square and skirted the Alexandrovski Sad park along the west side of the Kremlin. They entered at the Borovitskij Gate, went up the cobblestoned incline there without loss of pace and drew up before the Bolshoi Kremlevski Dvorets, the Great Kremlin Palace.

Two sentries snapped to attention as they entered. Evidently Frol's guards needed no passes. A sixteen-step ornate staircase led them up from the ground floor to a gigantic vestibule the vault of which was supported by four monolithic granite columns. They turned left and entered an anteroom. More guards who snapped to attention.

One of Frol Krasnaya's escort approached a heavy door

59

and knocked discreetly. Someone came, opened it slightly, evidently said something to someone else back in the room and then opened it widely enough for Krasnaya and his goons.

Inside, at a desk, sat a lean, competent and assured type who jittered over a heavy sheaf of papers with an electro-marking computer pen. He was nattily and immaculately dressed and smoked his cigarette in one of the small pipelike holders once made *de rigueur* through the Balkans by Marshall Tito.

The three of them came to a halt before his desk and, at long last, expression came to the faces of the zombis. Respect, with possibly an edge of perturbation, Here, obviously, was authority.

He at the desk finished a paper, tore it from the sheaf, pushed it into the maw of the desk chute. Then, to Frol Krasnaya's astonishment, the other came to his feet, quickly, smoothly and with a grin on his face. Frol hadn't considered the possibility of being grinned at in the Ministry of Internal Affairs.

"Aleksander Kardelj," the other said in self-introduction, sticking out a lean hand to be shaken. "You're Krasnaya, eh? We've been waiting for you."

Frol shook, bewildered. He looked at the zombi next to him, uncomprehendingly.

He who had introduced himself darted a look of comprehension from Frol to the two. He said, disgustedly but with mild humor oddly mixed, "What's the matter, did these hoodlums frighten you?"

Frol fingered his chin nervously. "Of course not."

One of the zombis shifted his feet. "We did nothing but obey orders."

Kardelj grimaced in sour amusement. "I can imagine," he grunted. "Milka, you see too many of these imported Tri-Di shows from the West. I suspect you see yourself

60

as a present-day Soviet Complex G-Man, or possibly James Bond, the Third."

"Yes, Comrade," Milka said, and then shook his head.

"Oh hush up and get out," Kardelj said. He flicked the cigarette butt from its holder with a thumb and took up a fresh one from a desk humidor and wedged it into the small bowl. He looked at Frol again and grinned.

"You can't imagine how pleased I am to meet you, at last," he said, "I've been looking for you for months."

Frol Krasnaya ogled him. The name had come through at last. Aleksander Kardelj was seldom in the news, practically never photographed and then in the background in a group of Party functionaries, usually with a wry smile on his face. But he was known throughout the wide boundaries of the Soviet Complex, if not internationally. Aleksander Kardelj, a Hungarian, was Number Two. Right-hand man of Andrei Zorin himself, second in command of the Party and rumored to be the brains behind the throne.

The Zombis had gone hurriedly.

"Looking for me?" Frol said blankly. "I haven't been in hiding. You've made some mistake. All I am is the junior *Pravda* reporter assigned to Greater Washington. I——"

"Of course, of course," Kardelj said, humorously impatient. He took up a folder from his desk and shook it absently in Frol's general direction. "I've studied your dossier thoroughly." He flicked his eyes up at a wall clock. "Come along. Comrade Zorin is expecting us."

In a daze, Frol Krasnaya followed him.

Comrade Zorin. Number One. Andrei Zorin, Secretary General of the Party, Chairman of the Presidium of the Central Committee. The heir of Lenin, Stalin, Khrushchev, Kosygin, and the other dictators of the Soviet Complex.

Frol could hardly remember so far back that Zorin wasn't head of the party, when his face, or sculptured bust, wasn't to be seen in every store, on the walls of banks, railroad stations, or bars. Never a newsreel but that part of it wasn't devoted to Comrade Zorin, never a Tri-Di newscast but that Number One was brought to the attention of the viewers.

Frol Krasnaya followed Kardelj in a daze through a door to the rear of the desk, and into a somewhat bigger room, largely barren of furniture save for a massive table with a dozen chairs about it. At the table, looking some ten years older than in any photo Frol had ever seen, sat Andrei Zorin.

He looked ten years older and his face bore a heavy weariness, a grayness, that never came through in his publicity shots. He looked up from a report and grunted a welcome to him.

Kardelj said in pleasurable enthusiasm, "Here his is, Andrei. The average young man of the whole Soviet Complex."

Number One grunted again and took in the less than imposing figure of Frol Krasnaya. Frol felt an urge to nibble at his fingernails and repressed it.

Andrei Zorin growled an invitation for them to be seated and Kardelj adjusted his trousers to preserve the crease, threw one leg up along the heavy conference table and rested on one buttock, looking at ease but as though ready to take off instantly.

Frol fumbled himself into one of the sturdy oaken chairs, staring back and forth at the two most powerful men of his native land. Thus far, no one had said anything that made any sense whatsoever to him since he had been hauled from his bed, two hours and more ago, in the Soviet Embassy of Greater Washington.

Zorin rasped, "I have gone through your dossier, Com-

rade. I note that you are the son of Hero of the People's
Democratic Dictatorship, Alex Krasnaya."

"Yes, Comrade Zorin," Frol got out.

Number One grunted. "I knew Alex well. You must
realize that his arrest was before my time. It was, of
course, after my election that he was exonerated and
his name restored to the list of those who have gloriously
served the State."

It wasn't exactly the way Frol knew the story, but he
simply nodded. He said, unhappily, "Comrades, I have
no idea . . ."

Kardelj was chuckling, as though highly pleased with
some development. He held up a hand to cut Frol short
and turned to his superior. "You see, Andrei. A most
average, laudable young man. Born under our regime,
raised under the People's Democratic Dictatorship of the
Soviet Complex. Exactly our man."

Zorin seemed not to hear the other. He was studying
Frol heavily, all but gloomily.

A beefy paw went out and banged a button inset in
the table and which Frol had not seen before. Almost
instantly a door in the rear opened and a white jacketed
servant entered pushing a wheeled combination bar and
hors d'oeuvres cart before him. He brought the lavishly
laden wagon to within reach of the heavyset Party head,
then made himself scarce.

Number One's heavy lips moved in and out as his eyes
went over the display.

Kardelj said easily, "Let me, Andrei." He arose and
brought a towel-wrapped bottle from a refrigerated buck-
et set into the wagon and deftly took up a delicate
three-ounce glass which he filled and placed before his
superior.

"Have one yourself," Zorin grunted.

Kardelj smiled in self-deprecation. "Not for me, Andrei.

Too weak a stomach for this strong stuff. For me, occasionally a glass of Georgian wine, or perhaps one of kvas from Uzbec."

Zorin grunted, "You don't know kvas from your elbow, Aleksander. I was raised on the stuff." His eyes piggish, he took up a heavy slice of dark bread and ladled a full quarter pound of caviar upon it, grunted and stuffed the open sandwich into his mouth.

He looked at Frol. "Comrade, I am not surprised at your confusion. We will get to the point. Actually, you must consider yourself a very fortunate young man." He belched, took another bite, and went on, "Have you ever heard the term expediter?"

"I . . . I don't think so, Comrade Zorin."

The Party head poured himself some more spirits. "Comrade Kardelj first came upon the germ of this idea of ours through reading of American industrial successes during the Second World War. They were attempting to quadruple their production of war materials in months. Obviously, a thousand bottlenecks appeared, so they resorted to expediters. Competent efficiency engineers whose sole purpose was to seek out such bottlenecks and eliminate them. A hundred aircraft might be kept from completion by the lack of a single part. The expediters found them though they be as far away as England, and flew them by chartered plane to California. I need give no further examples. Their powers were sweeping. Their expense accounts unlimited. Their successes unbelievable." Number One's eyes went back to the piles of food, as though he had grown tired of so much talk.

Frol figited, still uncomprehending.

While the Party leader built himself another huge sandwich, Aleksander Kardelj put in an enthusiastic word. "We're adapting the ideas to our own needs, Comrade. You have been selected to be our first expediter."

64

"Expediter? To . . . to expedite *what?*"

"That is for you to decide," Kardelj said blithely. "You are our average citizen. You feel as the man on the street feels. You're our, what the Yankees call, Common Man."

Frol said plaintively, "But I don't know what you mean, Comrade. What is this about me being, uh, the average man? There's nothing special about me."

"Exactly," Kardelj said triumphantly. "There's nothing special about you. You're the average man of all the Soviet Complex. We have gone to a great deal of difficulty to seek you out."

Number One belched and took over heavily. "Comrade, we have made extensive tests in this effort to find our average man. You are the result. You are of average age, of average weight, height, of education and of intelligence quotient. Your tastes, your ambitions, your . . . dreams, Comrade Krasnaya, are either known to be, or assumed to be, those of the average citizen." He took up a rich baklava dessert, saturated with honey, and devoured it.

Andrei Zorin took up a paper. "I have here a report from a journalist of the West who but recently returned from a tour of the Soviet Complex. She reports, with some indignation, that the only available eyebrow pencils were to be found on the black market, were of French import, and cost twenty rubles apiece. She contends that Soviet women are indignant at paying such prices."

The Party head looked hopelessly at first Frol and then Kardelj. "What is an eyebrow pencil?"

Frol took courage. He flustered. "They use it to darken their eyebrows—women, I mean. It comes and goes in popularity."

Karadelj said triumphantly, "See what I mean, Andrei? He's priceless."

Zorin looked at his right-hand man. "Why, if our women desire this . . . this eyebrow pencil nonsense, is it not supplied them? Is there some ingredient we don't produce? If so, why cannot it be imported?" He picked at his uneven teeth with a thumbnail.

Kardelj held his lean hands up, as though in humorous supplication. "Because, Comrade, to this point we have not had expediters to find out such desires."

Number One grunted and took up another report. "Here we have some comments upon service in our restaurants. This Western writer contends that the fact we have no tipping leads our waiters to be surly and inefficient. The tourist trade is important." He glowered across at Frol. "Typical of the weaknesses you must ferret out, Comrade."

He put the reports down with a grunt. "But these are comparatively minor. Last week a truck driver attached to a meat-packing house in Kiev was instructed to deliver a load. When he arrived it was to find they had no refrigeration facilities. So he unloaded the frozen meat on a warehouse platform and returned to Kiev. At this time of the year, obviously, in four hours the meat was spoiled." He glowered at Kardelj and then at Frol. "Why do things like this continually happen? How can we think we have overtaken the West when on all levels our workers are afraid to take initiative? He delivered the meat. He washed his hands of what happened afterwards. Why, Comrades? Why did he not have the enterprise to preserve his valuable load, even, if necessary, make the decision to return with it to Kiev?"

He grunted heavily and settled back as though through, finished with the whole question.

Aleksander Karedlj became brisk. "This is your job. You are to travel about the country, finding bottlenecks, finding shortages, ferreting out mistakes and bringing them to the attention of those in position to rectify them."

Frol said, "But suppose . . . suppose they ignore my findings?"

Number One snorted, but said nothing.

Kardelj said jovially, "Tomorrow the announcements will go out to every man, woman and child in the People's Democratic Dictatorship. Your word is law. You are answerable only to Comrade Zorin and myself. No restrictions whatsoever apply to you. No laws. No regulations. We will give you identication which all will recognize, and the bearer of which can do no wrong."

Frol was flabbergasted. "But . . . suppose I come up against some, well, someone high in the Party, or, well, some general, or admiral?"

Kardelj said jocularly, "You answer only to us. Your power is limitless. Comrade Zorin did not exaggerate. Frankly, were cold statistics enough, the Soviet Complex has already overtaken the West in per capita production, particularly in view of the depression now hitting them. Steel, agriculture, coal mined, petroleum pumped. All these supposed indications of prosperity. Why, our porpoise program is far and beyond theirs. We've not only taught *our* porpoises, based in the Sea of Okhotsk, to speak Russian, but to read in the Cyrillic alphabet. Beginning next week there will be a special edition of *Pravda* printed for them on plastic." He flung up his hands again, in his semi-humorous gesture of despair. "But all these things do not mesh. We cannot find such a simple matter as . . . as eyebrow pencils in our stores, nor can we be served acceptably in our restaurants and hotels. Each man passes the buck, as the Yankees say. No man wants responsibility."

"But . . . but me . . . only me. What could you expect a single person to do?"

"Don't misunderstand. You are but an experiment. If it works out, we will seek others who are also deemed potential expediters, to do similar work."

Frol said carefully, "From what you say, I . . . I can override anyone in the Soviet Complex, except yourselves. But what if I antagonize one of you? You know, with something I think I find wrong?"

The second in command of the Party chuckled, even as he fitted a fresh cigarette into his curved holder. "We've provided even for that, Comrade. Fifty thousand Common Europe francs have been deposited to your account in Switzerland. At any time you feel your revelations might endanger yourself, you are free to leave the country and achieve sanctuary abroad." He chuckled whimsically again. "Given the position you will occupy, a man above all law, with the whole of the nation's resources at his disposal, I cannot imagine you wishing to leave. The Swiss deposit is merely to give you complete confidence, complete security."

Chapter Eight

Weigand Patrick, standing at the side of the bed, looked down in open admiration. He said, "Now that's what I call table stuff. Turn over."

"No," Scotty said into the large pillow where she had burrowed her head.

"Why not?"

"I'm embarrassed."

"Embarrassed! After the type clothes you wear around all day? Or, rather, don't wear."

Scotty said, her voice muffled, "I've never been in a man's bed before."

He sat on the edge of it and reached out a hand.

"Hey," she said. "Cut that out! What do you think I am, a sailor?"

He said, "This is what's known as preliminary sex play. It's in all the instruction manuals. You gotta have sex play."

"Oh yeah. Well, play somewhere else."

"Here?"

She drew in her breath. "That's . . . different."

"You mean better?"

"I said, different."

"Turn over."

"Turn out the lights."

"Why? I want to see you. I'm hung up on redheads. It runs in the family, my old man's life-long ambition was to go to bed with a redheaded woman in black underwear. But he never did."

"Why not?" her voice was intrigued.

"My mother wouldn't let him. Turn over."

She said into the pillow, "Have you got your clothes off?"

"Yes."

She dug her head further into the pillow.

"I'm wearing pajamas," he said.

She half turned, indignantly. "How come you insist I be stark naked and you wear pajamas?" Then her eyes widened, accusingly. "You're only wearing the *tops*."

"That's all I ever wear," he said, reaching for her. "Now about this preliminary sex play. First, we start here . . ."

Her eyes rolled up and her mouth went slack.

The phone screen buzzed.

"Holy smokes!" he protested.

"What's that?" she muttered.

"My private line to the White House."

"Well . . . stop doing that . . . for a minute. You . . . you'd better answer it'"

"No. Damn it."

"Stop doing that, WeeWee Patrick. Take your head away. That's not what you're supposed to do anyway . . . I'm sure. You'd better answer it. It's probably some emergency."

"Of course it's an emergency. It's always an emergency. Let somebody else worry about it."

She sat up abruptly. "You'll *have* to answer it. I couldn't concentrate, anyway. Knowing some emergency was on."

"Not even if I did this?"

Her eyes rolled up again. "You cut that out, you queer, and go answer the phone. Tell them you're sick, or something. Refer them to Fred Moriarty."

"Ha," he grumbled. "That bastard's trying to get my job." He sat erect on the bed's edge and glowered at the still buzzing phone screen.

"Well, you don't want the job, anyway."

"I don't know," he said lowly, still glaring at the device which was attempting to summon him. "There's an awful lot of unemployment in this country, and presidential assistants aren't that much in demand."

"I thought you were a newspaperman."

"Newspaperman, for God's sake? Do you know how many newspapermen are still working? The publishers have finally gone the whole hog. *The New York Times* has amalgamated with *The Los Angeles Times*. They met in Kansas City and assimilated the *Star* while they were at it."

He came to his feet, in disgust, and moved toward the phone screen.

"Hey," Scotty said. "Don't turn that thing on, until I get out of the way."

Weigand leered at her over his shoulder. "Why not? I'd like the word to get around, the high quality stuff I get into my bed. A reputation like that and all the broads start wondering just what it is you have. Your reputation gets big enough and you can't fight them off. Look at Don Juan, look at Casanova, look at Rubirosa. They didn't know what hit 'em. Look at that old timer Tommy Manville."

"Yeah, Tommy Manville," she sneered. "He inherited Ponce DeLeon's pants."

"Ponce DeLeon's pants?"

"The old jerk who explored Florida looking for the Fountain of Youth. He was just about to bathe in it, when the Indians raided. His pants fell in. He fished them out. Then had to beat a retreat."

He scowled at her, looked over at the screen, looked back. "What the hell are you talking about, at a time like this?"

"Ponce DeLeon's pants. So long as you wore them, you were hot for everybody. But then . . ."

He got it. "When you took them off . . ." He shook his head. "That's the kind of girl I fall for. What a mind. I bet you made that up on the spur of the moment."

He turned the instrument so that the screen faced a different corner of the room, and sat down before it. He flicked the switch.

It was Fred Moriarty.

Fred said, "Where were you? I was about to try somewhere else."

"I'm here," Weigand said disgustedly. "What the hell is it? I'm busy. Or, at least, want to be."

The Presidential Appointment Secretary said, "Wei-

71

gand, you'd better get over here soonest. I've got something I'm not sure I know how to handle."

"Sounds like this new strain of clap. What?"

"An inventor that's been trying to get in to see the Chief for the past couple of weeks."

"Well, why didn't you let him? God knows, the Sachem'll see just about anybody these days, hoping something'll come up."

"I thought he was a crackpot."

"All right, then send him over to the Office of Science and Technology, Crackpot Division, or whatever they call that department that investigates new inventions."

Fred Moriarty's face was harried. "I was going to, but he wouldn't take the brush-off. He didn't want to show his damn invention to anybody but the President, but finally, kind of in despair, he showed it to me."

Weigand Patrick was beginning to become intrigued.

From the bed, Scotty, in an urgent whisper, said, "Look, either perform or get off the pot. Are you coming back, or not?"

"Shhh," he said, over his shoulder. "Just a minute."

He turned back to the phone screen and his colleague. "Well, what is the big invention?"

"I can't tell you over the phone."

Weigand Patrick looked at him. "This is a special line."

"I don't care. Lines have been tapped before."

"Well, give me a hint."

"I can't."

"Well, where is this crackpot inventor?"

"I've got two of the Secret Service boys guarding him."

"Holy smokes," Weigand said. "You really have got maiden aunts in your pants. Can't you give me any idea of what the invention will do?"

Fred Moriarty said very slowly, "If I'm any judge, it

72

will boom the Chief's popularity poll rating to 95 percent, overnight."

"Ninety-five percent! Do you know what it is now?"

"There isn't any now."

"Ninety-five percent!"

Fred Moriarty said very slowly, "It is estimated that the agnostics and athiests in this country number five percent of the population. We'll get everybody else."

"Holy smokes."

"You're telling me."

"I'll be right over!" He slammed off the switch of the phone screen, got up and hurried in the direction of his clothes.

Scotty looking at him from the bed, blinked and said, "Where did it go?"

"What?" he said absently, struggling into his shirt.

"That . . . that thing."

He said hurriedly, "Look, honey, I've got to make a bee-line over to the White House."

"What for?"

"I don't know."

She stared at him in indignation. "You mean to tell me, you bring me here and then before you even get started you have to dash off on some silly errand for Old Chucklehead?" She said suspiciously, "That was Fred Moriarty. What's going on?"

"Evidently, something so secret that he was afraid to tell me on the phone," Weigand said, struggling into his pants.

She said, "I didn't know they went away like that."

"What went away?"

"You know."

"Honey, there's a lot of things you obviously don't know. It will be my greatest privilege to teach you,

73

later." He added, as an inducement, "They only go away temporarily." He added, indignantly, "Besides, it didn't go away, it just shrunk, kind of."

"Are you coming back later? Should I wait?"

He rolled his eyes upward and groaned in pure misery. "I guess not. I have a sneaking suspicion that this particular emergency is going to string on for awhile."

In the outer office to the presidential study, Fred Moriarty was waiting for him.

"Well," Weigand Patrick snapped, "where is he?"

"I've got him in your office, with Steve and Wes guarding him."

"Is he that tough? What was he trying to get at the Sachem for? What the hell is this invention, anyway?" Weigand Patrick looked sardonic. "Or do you think this office might be bugged too?"

A flicker of apprehension passed over the appointment secretary's face, but then he shook his head. "You'll have to see on your own."

Weigand turned, "Well, let's go, then."

"Not me."

Weigand turned back and stared, "What'd'ya mean, not you?"

"I've seen it, and it gives me the shakes."

"By God, this place is turning into a nut factory. I wish the hell I'd become a Baptist missionary like my dear old mother wanted." He turned back to the door again.

Fred Moriarty said urgently, "Don't let Steve and Wes be there when he demonstrates it."

Weigand Patrick was staring again. "Why not?"

"It's the toppest secret there's ever been. This secret makes the Manhattan Project look like a Women's Sunday Afternoon Bridge and Gossip Society."

"Jesus H. Christ," Weigand said. He turned and left Fred Moriarty's office and headed for his own in the White House west wing.

Steve Hammond was standing outside Patrick's office door, his right hand under his jacket lapel.

Weigand snapped at him, "What the hell's going on?"

"Yes, sir, Mr. Patrick. Mr. Moriarty's instructions. The subject is inside. Wes is on guard in there."

"Does this guy look as dangerous as all that?"

"Well, no sir. From what Mr. Moriarty says, *he's* not dangerous. Mr. Moriarty says just to be sure that nobody gets to him—except you, of course, Mr. Patrick."

"Thanks," Weigand said. He pushed open the door of his office and entered.

The office of Weigand Patrick, press secretary, special assistant, right-hand man, and operational brains of the President of the United States of the Americas, had been decorated to its occupant's tastes. There was a very large desk, fouled high with everything that a desk could conceivably accumulate. There was a small bar in the corner. There were book shelves, filled with an assortment less orthodox than might be expected in a bureaucrat of his ranking. There were half a dozen very comfortable chairs, and what Weigand called his casting couch.

In one of the very comfortable chairs sat an unknown. He was about five-foot four, would go perhaps a hundred and fifteen pounds, carrying a suitcase and after being caught out in the rain, and wore a lost pup expression. His scrawny beard gave the impression that moths not only made a custom of bedding down in it, but carousing there.

Weigand Patrick looked first at him, then at the Secret Service man who had scrambled to his feet at

75

Weigand's slamming entrance. He had been seated in the ultra-comfortable upholstered swivel chair which was the press secretary's pride and often joy.

"Wes," Weigand smiled benignly at the bodyguard, "if I ever catch you in my chair again, I'll have you shot at dawn on the Octagon paradeground, after having had utilized on you some of the Nazi war surplus they have over in the museum there." He added, gently, "Do you doubt I could have that done, Wes?"

"Well, no sir," the other blurted. "But I don't think the President would like that, Mr. Patrick."

"To the contrary, the way he's feeling these days, I think he'd be over to watch when they got around to those testicle squeezers. Get the hell out of here."

"Yes, sir. I'll be at the door, Mr. Patrick." He got.

Weigand Patrick looked at the other occupant of the office. He said, "I'm Weigand Patrick. It's been said that I pinch hit for Horace Adams, under certain circumstances."

"Newton Brown," the other said, bobbing his adam's apple, and blinking at the door through which the Secret Service man had just exited. "My friends call me Newt."

"I'll bet they do." Weigand went over to the bar. "Would you like a drink?"

"Well . . . do you know how to mix a John Brown's Body?"

"A John Brown's Body? What are its essentials, and what do they do to you?"

The little man nodded. "That's a good question," he said. "Too many people don't ask. Frankly, in the morning you feel like you're moldering in your grave. I named the concoction after an ancestor. The ingredients are an egg, rum, absinthe, metaxa and pulque."

"Pulque?"

"Pulque. I have to have mine shipped up specially

76

from Mexico. You can substitute dark beer, but it's not the same."

"Dark beer we have," Weigand said, miffed. He prided himself on his bar. He made a mental note to order some pulque.

He mixed, taking the other's instructions as he went. Eventually, they wound up, tall glasses in hand, facing each other, Weigand behind his desk.

Weigand Patrick sipped his and said, "Holy Smokes."

"Good, aren't they?" the other beamed.

Weigand peered down into his glass. "What happened to the eggshell? I never heard of dropping an eggshell into a drink before."

"Gives calcium to your system," Newton Brown said. "It's usually dissolved by this time."

Weigand Patrick coughed. "Okay," he said. "So much for the amenities. I understand you're an inventor."

"That is correct, sir." The other sighed. "I might almost say, the last of the traditional inventors. The posterity of the inventor of yesteryear, a descendent of the alchemist of old, if you will, who worked in his own garret; of the talented tinkerer of old, who had his laboratory in cellar, or, later, garage. Today . . ." the little man sighed ". . . inventions are made in assembly-line laboratories where a scientist might not even know the nature of the final product upon which he is expanding his cerebral labors."

Weigand ignored the fruity language. "Newton Brown, Newton Brown," he said. "The name escapes me. I don't believe I have ever heard of any of your own particular, ah, breakthroughs."

Newton Brown finished off his drink, without a flinch, and handed his glass over to his host, rather than putting it down.

He sighed. "No, I suppose not. Most of my work has been suppressed, one way or the other."

"Suppressed?"

"That is correct." He brought a wallet from his clothes, fished around in it and handed Weigand Patrick a slip of yellow paper.

Weigand, scowling, the empty glass still held in his right hand, looked at it. "Fifty thousand dollars. Holy Smokes!" It was a check from the Associated Towel Manufacturers of the United Americas.

"It's always like that," the little man was complaining. "Something always happens to my work, it never reaches the public. I can't afford not to take this check, and obviously now they'll suppress it."

"Who'll suppress what?" Weigand Patrick said, staring at the pleasant sum.

"The Associated Towel Mnaufacturers," Newt Brown sighed. "They're just bought up my dry water discovery."

Weigand looked at him.

"Dry water, dry water," Brown repeated. "Endless possibilities, obviously. Absolutely revolutionize irrigation. Carry it around in burlap bags. Also, veterinarians expressed an interest, for washing animals such as cats who don't like to get wet. I stumbled upon it while experimenting with *light* water. I'm very much a basic research scientist, you know. Pure research. Science for science's sake. All that sort of thing." He added, sadly, "Quite a genius."

Weigand got to his feet and went over and concocted the concoction again. He brought the two drinks back and handed one of them to the other.

He said, cautiously, "What did you figure *light* water would do?"

The other sipped his drink appreciatively and leaned

78

forward as though confidential. "You've heard of *heavy* water, obviously? Well, I concluded that if I could devise a *light* water it would revolutionize reducing and end obesity overnight." For a moment the little man seemed inspired in his dream. His eyes brightened.

"I . . . I don't believe I get you," Weigand said.

"Obvious," Newt Brown said. "You must know that at least ninety percent of the human body is composed of water. Well, if I could substitute *light* water for regular H_2O in a person's chemical make-up, he'd weigh considerably less. Simple, isn't it?"

For a brief moment, Weigand Patrick let his mind consider some of the ramifications. Then he shook his head for clarity, and looked down into his drink again, accusation there.

"Not exactly," he said. "But what happened to your light water experiments?"

"Oh, you government people suppressed them. Some bureau or other, I forget which one."

"The government?" Weigand scowled. He had almost certainly never heard of Newton Brown before.

The little man nodded earnestly. "As you undoubtedly know, heavy water is extremely important in nuclear fission. Well . . . it's obvious, isn't it? One experiment leads to another and I was beginning to dabble in reverse nuclear fission with my light water, when they clamped down on me."

"Reverse nuc . . ."

But Brown held up a restraining hand. "Sorry, but I have given my word not to discuss it. Undoubtedly, you are in a position to be cleared for this information. But until you are, and until I have received permission to . . ."

"All right, all right. You seem to be in quite a rut,"

Weigand said. He was beginning to feel the drink—if you could call it a drink. "First it's dry water, then it's light water."

The other retrieved his check and put it back in his wallet with a sigh. "The compound has always fascinated me. There should be *some* sensible use for it—obviously it's a flop as a beverage."

Weigand Patrick said sarcastically, "Have you given any thought to black water?"

"Black water? It's possible advantageousness seems to elude me."

"Maybe for people who don't care if they're dirty or not, to wash with."

Newton Brown blinked at him. "I fear you jest."

"Yeah, maybe," Weigand Patrick said in resignation. "Look, let's get to the point. The president's appointment secretary seems to think you have some, well, rather far-out invention. He tells me you have been trying to get to the President with it."

"Ah, well yes."

"Okay. What is it?"

Newton Brown pursed his lips. "Perhaps I could best illustrate by stating that I am spiritually opposed, morally opposed, to the present stance of President Horace Adams' in containing Finland and conducting the police action in the Antarctic."

Actually, Weigand felt the same way; however, it wasn't his branch of responsibility. He said blandly, "However, Mr. Brown, I am afraid your opinions are not those of the most farsighted, the most highly informed and the most spiritually oriented . . ."

Weigand Patrick broke off in mid-sentence and his eyes bugged as they had never bugged in the thirty-odd years of the existence of Weigand Patrick.

For above the head of Newton Brown, frustrated inventor extraordinary, there floated what would only be described by the most negatively prejudiced as a halo.

It was a halo as painted by the most delicate masters of the Renaissance, a vertiable soft rainbow of a halo. There were mother-of-pearl aspects, too. It was possibly the single most beautiful thing that Weigand Patrick had ever seen in his life. It was faint, it was delicate; but there were no two ways about it. Newton Brown had a halo over his head.

Weigand said shakily, "Excuse me." Taking his glass over to the small sink that was part of the bar, he poured the rest of his drink down.

On second thought, he took up a bottle of twelve-year-old Irish, poured a triple slug, and knocked it back.

His grandparents had been religious but not since them had the family given much thought to the here-after and related subjects. He came back and sat down again and looked at his guest. The halo was gone. However, Weigand Patrick was still shaken.

He said, "Look. I respect your . . . ah, spiritual opinions."

Newton Brown said nothing.

Weigand Patrick said carefully. "However, uh . . . well, the President's position on his international stands are . . . well . . . of the highest moral . . ."

"I think they're unholy . . ."

The halo faded in again, above Newton Brown's head.

Weigand Patrick had come back to his swivel chair. He got up again and went back to the bar and poured himself another double Irish in a daze. He knocked it back. He returned to his desk.

He said, "Uh, I am not very well . . . That is, I am not very spiritually, uh, oriented." Happily, the halo was gone.

The other's drink was gone. He said, "I beg your par-

81

don?" holding his glass out in the obvious need for a refill.

Weigand said, "I . . . well, I suppose I've neglected my religious obligations. Only this evening I . . . well, that's not important. The thing is, I've never thought in terms before . . . that is, not until now . . . of, of well, taking holy orders . . ."

Newton Brown said interestedly, "You know, that was the first response of your colleague, this Frederick Moriarty."

"I'll bet it was," Weigand muttered. "Look, I'm not feeling exactly . . . I think I better get in touch with the staff psychiatrist and . . ."

"Oh, that won't be necessary."

"What do you know about it?" Weigand all but snarled. "I know when I'm not feeling well. Besides, I think I've been drinking too much . . . or something."

"I'll show you how it works," the other said reasonably.

Weigand Patrick looked at him. "How what works?"

Newton Brown brought an object from his pocket. It looked like a rather elaborate cigarette case with a button on the side. "I call it the Aurora Borealis," he said. "Makes it easier for the layman to comprehend."

"You call *what* the Aurora Borealis? Listen, you'll never believe this, but you know that I thought I saw a . . ."

Newt Brown interrupted by ostentatiously pushing the button on the seeming cigarette case. The halo was there, above his head. He let the button off, the halo was gone.

Weigand Patrick bug-eyed again.

The little inventor handed him the cigarette case. "It's not at all as complicated as you might think. The fact is, scientists have known for some time that every human being—every animal for that matter—has a magnetic-electric aura about them. Invisible, of course. Something like the electric fields which surround the Earth and are especially prevalent at the North and South poles. Discharges of ions through this aura are what causes the so beautiful Aurora Borealis, the so-called Northern Lights. Now, what I've done——"

"Wait a minute now, you've lost me. What I want to know is . . . this damn thing . . . it'll work on anybody?"

"Of course. Try it."

Weigand swallowed and pressed the button. Nothing seemed to happen.

Newt Brown said in satisfaction, "Of course. Anybody at all. Looks very good on you. Rather dashing."

Weigand Patrick stumbled to his feet and made his way to the small bathroom connected with his office. He stared into the mirror above the lavatory.

He said, "I'm a saint," and pushed the button.

The halo was there.

Newt Brown was correct. On him, it looked rather dashing. As though he was some medieval warrior-saint, somebody like Sir Galahad.

Weigand Patrick stared at his image and muttered, meaninglessly, "His strength was as the strength of ten, because his heart was pure."

He returned to his desk and sat the cigarette case down very carefully. He looked at Newt Brown, who was wearing a smirk, and said, "You mean this thing will work for anybody at all?"

"Like I said, even animals have the invisible magnetic-electric aura. All my device does is power it."

"You mean," Weigand demanded, "even a jackass, if he pressed this button, would have a halo around his head?"

"Well, I don't know how a jackass could press a button, is all."

"Well, I do," Weigand muttered. "Just a minute. Let

me think, damn it." He ran a hand over his chin nervously. "I've got to think about this."

He turned suddenly to his phone screen, flicked it on and snapped, "Mr. Moriarty's office."

When Fred Moriarty faded in on the screen, Weigand snapped, without preliminaries, "Listen, the Tri-Di speech the Sachem is going to make. That revival of President Roosevelt's Fireside Chat . . ."

"I know," Fred said. "I'm way ahead of you."

"Every time he makes one of those cornball platitudes the speechwriting boys have been digging up, like: *All we have to fear, is fear itself*, and *a chicken in every pot——*"

"I'm way ahead of you," Fred Moriarty repeated.

Weigand Patrick said despeartely, "Listen, have you mentioned this to anybody at all? *Anybody* . . . ?"

"No. Nobody but you . . ."

"Hang on," Weigand said. "Don't leave your office." He flicked off the phone screen and spun on Newton Brown. He leveled a finger at the inventor, who was beginning to show nervous symptoms. "How many people know about this device? How many have you demonstrated it to?"

Newt Brown swallowed. "I work alone. Veritable hermit . . . so to speak. Tradition of the alchemists and all that——"

"Answer me, dammit!"

"Nobody," Newt Brown protested. "Nobody but you and Mr. Frederick Moriarty."

Weigand came to his feet, went to the office door, opened it and called, "Steve, Wes, in here on the double."

The two efficient looking Secret Service men came darting through the door.

Weigand Dennis pointed at Newton Brown. "That man

is the biggest potential threat to the President's security in the country. Guard him with your lives!"

With a squeal, Newt Brown was out of his chair and scurrying for the door, zig-zagging between the three larger men.

He almost made it. Steve Hammond flicked a blackjack from a hip pocket and took a swing at him as he passed, and missed. Wes, now in a gunfighter's crouch, blurred into motion and magically there was a .357 Caliber Magnum in his hand.

"Clear out of the way," Wes yelled. "I'll nail him."

However, Weigand Patrick had stuck a foot out, tripping up the desperate little man, so that he smashed, face first, into the rug.

While the two burly Secret Service men grabbed him up by both arms, Weigand Patrick glared at them. "Holy Smokes, I said *guard*, not kill him." But then he twisted his face in thought. "Although, come to think of it, maybe that'd be the easiest thing."

"Help," Newt Brown squealed. "Police!"

"Shut up!" Weigand said. "I've got to think." He went back to his bar and took down another slug of the Irish. It didn't seem to have any effect.

He turned finally to the two Secret Service men. "Take him over to Blair House and stick him in the south suite. You're not to leave him, night or day. And nobody else is to get near him. Above all, don't let him talk to anybody. If anybody trys to talk to him, shoot them."

Steve Hammond said briskly, "Nobody talks to him but us, eh?"

A new thought came to Weigand Patrick and he glared. "Listen," he said. "The same thing applies to you two. You don't talk to him, either. Steve, if Wes talks to this man, shoot Wes; Wes, if Steve talks to him, shoot Steve."

The little man said pathetically, "Suppose I have to go to the bathroom, or something?"

"Use sign language," Weigand snapped. "All right, get out of here."

When they were gone, he stared down at his desk for awhile. Finally, he reached out and switched on the phone screen. It took a time to get the person he wanted.

When the other had faded in, he said, "Look, Edgar, what ever happened to that prison down on Dry Tortugas?"

"What prison?"

Weigand Patrick said impatiently, "Following the Civil War, and Lincoln's assassination, there was a lot of hushing up about the trial and the people involved with Booth. The doctor who had treated Booth was shipped down to that prison and spent the rest of his life there, the strictest orders being that he not be allowed to talk to anybody. Sort of a Man-In-the-Iron-Mask sort of thing."

The one on the screen said blankly, "What about it?"

Weigand Patrick said, "I have four men I want sent to that prison and kept there under the same circumstances. Absolutely no conversation with anybody at all, even prison guards."

The other could see it was obviously a matter of the highest security. In his day he had been a man of quick reactions, quick decisions.

"Very well," he snapped, his somewhat aged voice not quite cracking. "Who are the four?"

"Two of the President's Secret Service guards, Steve Hammond and Wes Fielding, and the man they're guarding, an inventor named Newton Brown."

"Got it, Weigand. And who is the fourth man we take down to Dry Tortugas?"

"Fred Moriarty."

Chapter Nine

The two were seated at the heavy mahogany table when the Professor bustled in, followed at a trot by his secretary, Walthers.

They had been killing time discussing the latest developments of Project Porpoise.

Les Frankle said, "That's what they get for teaching overgrown fish to talk."

Jimmy Leath said, "Porpoises aren't fish. They're mammals, like we are; and have as big a brain capacity. It's just that they live in the ocean, instead of on land. What's wrong with teaching them to talk?"

"First they wanted pay to keep track of the herds of meat whales, so the President sent them a committee of long-winded negotiaters, and gave them a long song and dance about the Wagner Act, or something. At any rate, now they've formed a union."

"Lads, lads," the Professor said jovially. "Let us be about business."

The two came to their feet until the roly-poly older man took a chair at the table's end.

At first glance, possibly owing to the similarity of their dress, they might have been taken for being from the same mold, but not at second. The thinnest was wry and bitter of face; the youngest, unsure and unhappy.

The Professor had an informal word for each of his youthful staff. "Well, James how is the ulcer? Are we still on milk?"

Jimmy Leath was still on milk.

The Professor turned to the other. "Lester, has Irene

convinced you as yet that you should resign from Doolittle Research and take a position a bit more, ah, worthy of your scholarly abilities?"

Les Frankle flushed. "Well, no sir, not yet."

The Professor smiled at him in fatherly condescension. "I can not quite see her point, lad. Where would your efforts gain greater remuneration than here? Especially in these days of unemployment."

Les squirmed. "Well, it's not that, Professor Doolittle. Irene's a do-gooder . . . well, in the best sense of the word. She thinks the fact that the best brains in the country are going into such fields as advertising, sales promotion, motivational research to learn how best to con the consumer . . ."

The Professor's shaggy white eyebrows went up. "Con?"

Les said apologetically, "A but of slang Irene used, sir. It's derived from confidence man."

"*Indeed.* So our crusader, Irene, lacks sympathy for our free enterprise society, eh? By George, where would you lads be, fresh out of the university, if there were not such organizations as Doolittle Research, ah, to take you in, and give you the opportunity to exercise your fledgling abilities?"

Les Frankle lacked the ability to dissimulate. He said earnestly, "Well, that's her point, sir. She says that such organizations as this take the country's best brains, use them while they're still fresh and trained in the latest techniques, then in a few years discard them for somebody younger and fresher. And by that time the individual is either disillusioned . . ." he looked at Jimmy ". . . or has ulcers, or is an alcoholic, or some such."

"A discouraging picture, By George," the Professor chuckled. "However, I suppose we should get to business lads."

He turned to Jimmy Leath. "So what have our depth interviews revealed in the way of an adult hero around whom we could build a fad to end all fads?" He added unctiously, "Thus helping to end the depression."

The emaciated psychologist bunched his right hand into a fist and rubbed it across his stomach. "On the first level of conscious, rational thought they think in terms of the president, or some top business figure, especially one who's worked his own way up. If you take in the past they'll come up with Lincoln, Washington, possibly Jesus."

Les grunted. "That's on the rational level," he muttered. "What happens when we get down to the preconscious, the subconscious?"

Jimmy looked at him and nodded. "Now, that's another thing. They'll run everywhere from some Tri-Di star, especially one who's hung on for a long time and always played sympathetic, masculine roles, to some military hero, ranging from Alexander to Custer."

The Professor was frowning, albeit benignly. "And when we get to the deepest levels of consciousness?"

Jimmy rubbed his stomach again and grimaced. "Billy the Kid, Wild Bill Hickok, Nero, the Marquis de Sade, Hitler——"

"Hitler!" Les Frankle ejaculated.

Jimmy nodded. "You'd be surprised how many can identify with someone who exercised absolute power."

The Professor said jovially, "Lads, lads, we are departing from reality. A gunman or a great sadist of the past, I hardly think would do."

Jimmy twisted in his chair and said, "What about Wyatt Earp? He was a gun thrower but usually on the side of the law."

"Usually, but not always," Les nodded. "I thought about him. A good muckraker would soon have our hero all dirtied up. Besides, he's old hat. He was on TV for years back before the depression."

"How about Daniel Boone?" Jimmy said.

"Too nearly like Davy Crockett. That Wild West that Was bit has been done too thoroughly," Les said. "At long last it's on it's way out."

"Amen," Jimmy murmured.

The Professor looked at him a bit testily. "Possibly you are correct James. But we have been weeks upon this, confound it. What is an alternative?"

Les said unhappily, "I thought of J.E.B. Stuart, the cavalry commander."

Jimmy said, "The military is always good. Half of the heroes our probes dug up were military. Lots of blood and guts."

The Professor said, "Lads, remember the requirements I gave you. This fad is for adults, By George, not children. I submit that if we made a Confederate general our hero we could sell toy sabers to children, Confederate grey uniforms and slouch hats. But that would be about it. Lads, let us start thinking *big*."

They sat in long silence.

The Professor looked at Les Frankle indulgently. "Well, Lester, where are these super-brains your good wife, Irene, complains that Doolittle Research is milking?"

Les colored and said unhappily, "Well, Irene had an idea."

"Irene! My dear Lester, I informed you of the high security nature of this project. By George, what would happen if the think tank's campaign were to be revealed before we even got underway? The public must think this fad spontaneous, By George, or it will never take!"

Les said, "I discuss all my work with Irene, sir. You've got to remember that she's a psychologist too. One of the best."

Jimmy said, soothing stomach pains with massage, "What'd she suggest? I still say some military figure."

"Her idea comes under that category—in a way," Les said. "Jeanne d'Arc."

"John Dark?" the Professor said, "Confound it, Lester, I've never even heard of the gentleman."

The two looked at him. Les smiled as though trying to be appreciative of a humorous sally. Jimmy closed his eyes, as though his ulcer was on campaign.

"Joan of Arc," Les said. He looked at Jimmy. "That gives you your military."

"A woman," Jimmy grumbled. "Not even a woman, a girl. I thought we were looking for a hero."

The Professor pursed plump lips. "Women spent some eighty percent of the average family income. Tell us more, Lester."

Les said, "Well, Irene thinks that Joan has just about everything." He looked at Jimmy again. "The muckrakers wouldn't be able to dig up much about her. She was only nineteen and a virgin when they burned her and there's a lot of sentimental pull in a martyr." He looked back at Professor Doolittle. "Irene says you could use her sword as a symbol."

"A symbol?"

"Irene says all big fads—or movements—have to have a symbol. Davy Crockett had the coonskin hat, the Nazis had their swastika. For that matter, the Mohammedans had their crescent and the Christians their cross."

The Professor said, "By George."

Jimmy growled, "What could you sell in the name of Joan of Arc?"

Warren Dempsey Witherson hacked his throat clear and said, "What could we sell, in the name of Joan of Arc?"

91

The Professor refreshed both their glasses. "Kid, you are not up on your history. She is a natural. She hasn't been done for decades in the movies. We shall have to do a super-spectacular, in the Tri-Di medium, this time. Some old playwright, Bernard Shaw, did a play on her. We shall revive it on Broadway and sent out three or four road shows to boot. Mark Twain wrote a biography of her, in fictional form. It is on the public domain. We shall issue it in a special deluxe limited edition, in regular hardcovers and finally in paperbacks. We shall line up a top dressing house in Paris and start off a Joan of Arc style revival. It is about time women got something brand new in the way of fashion. They can't think of anything else to reveal."

"There isn't anything else left to reveal," Warren Dempsey Witherson told him. "They've revealed everything."

"We'll hide it again," the Professor explained. "The Demure Look. Pageboy hair-do. Heather perfume. *Fleur-de-lis* designs on everything from textiles to earrings."

"Flour de lee?" Witherson said.

"It is kind of a design the old French kings used, according to one of my lads. That is just the beginning. Wait until we unleash all the boys. We shall start a Joan of Arc comic strip, of course. And Joan of Arc dolls for the tots. Then we will have to concoct some items for the Dauphin."

"The dolphin?" Witherson said blankly. "Dolphins are porpoises, aren't they? You mean we're even going to sell this fad to those talking fish they've been training to herd whales?"

"Dauphin, Dauphin, not dolphin. Jimmy Leath, one of my double-domed lads suggests we change history about a bit and make the French prince her boyfriend. Then we shall be able to cop a few scores from the men, too."

"Can we do that?" the aged grifter said nervously.

"Don't be a winchell, Kid. They made a hero out of Davy Crockett, did they not? Did you ever read a biography of that character? We can make a lover out of Charles, or whatever his name was."

Warren Dempsey Witherson looked at his long-time friend in admiration. "Where'd you get all this poop, Professor?"

Professor Doolittle was modest. "I have a secretary do up a brief from the Encyclopedia," he said. "I shall have it sent around to you."

"I guess I'll buy it, Professor," Witherson said finally. "I'll take the shuttle down to Greater Washington tomorrow. The President's having another brain trust meeting. The depression's getting worse by the minute. Then, given his approval, I'll lob over to Frisco and get the Oedipus Group, the businessman's think tank, to work. Anything special you can think of?"

"One thing. Have them line up every manufacturer in the country that is set to turn out swords."

Witherson blinked.

"Little decorative swords, scabbards and belts. A sword about two feet long. In every price range, from a few bucks up to bejeweled deals to go with evening wear— assume there are a few broads still in the country that can afford evening wear. It is our symbol, the sword. Kind of a crusader-like cross for a hilt and guard. You will have some boys in the ad outfits who will get the idea. We want to have the manufacturers all sewed up before the wisenheimers begin to jump on our bandwagon."

Chapter Ten

Old Sam, sprawled out on a park bench with several of his cronies, was saying, "You fellers expect too much from the govermint. It don't stand to experience to expect too much from the govermint. You never could." One of the others said, "Why, I dunno, Sam. Seems to me the govermint does pretty good. When I was a young- ster back into the first depression, if somebody doled out a bowl of watered down soup, all the newspapers yelled it was creeping socialism. Now maybe nine folks out of ten is on relief. What can you call that but progress?"

Sam said, "That ain't what I meant. Though I ain't saying this is a *better* depression than the last one. One thing, we didn't have inflation back them days. In fact, it was kinda the other way around. Things got cheaper. Everybody was going around shining shoes. There was three shoeshine men for every pair of shoes that was up to taking a shining. But what did they get? Five cents to shine a pair of shoes."

He motioned, with a sweeping gesture, at the several hundred shoeshine men who lined the edges of the park, none of them busy. "But then the govermint found out you didn't need any gold in Fort Knox to back up the money. All you needed was an automated printing press. Now we got inflation. Shoe shines, a dollar a throw. Sure, I admit, that's progress, it's a cry and shame to ask a growed man to shine shoes for five cents."

"Well, what did you mean?" one of the others yawned.

Sam said, "I mean you can't expect these govermint fellers to be smart. Too busy, for one thing. You take

94

into the Second War. When we first got into it, some big wheel in Washington, he figgered people wasn't war conscious enough, like they was over to England and France and all. So what did he figger out? He passed a rule against sliced bread. So everybody went out and had to buy bread knives so they could slice their own bread. And then about six months later, the govermint decided it was okay to slice bread again. The big emergency was over. So those bakeries that still had their old bread slicers, they oiled them up again and started slicing the bread. And the bakeries that didn't, they hadta buy new ones."

One of the others said, "I knowa better un than that. I was living out to California. In those days they was rationing gasoline like crazy. You hadta have coupons and all. Anyway, out in the oil country we was producing high octane gas for the war planes, and a by-product, like, of aviation gas, is white gas. They had white gas all over the place, and finally no place to store it all. So, do you think they give it out to the people? Shucks no, that ain't the govermint's style. They poured it out on the ground."

One of the oldsters squirmed in his seat in memory. "I was in England during the war. It wasn't so bad in England. Those Limeys are a caution. Talk about govermint fellers not being so smart. Those there Limeys were. They used to charge us Americans rent for the airfields we was flying from to protect London from the Messerschmidts and all."

Old Sam said, "That's where I was for a spell. England. Got good draft brew in England. The best is Bass Ale. I figure I musta drank three, four hogsheads of Bass Ale whilst I was to England."

The air force veteran was indignant. "You don't know Bass from a hole in the ground," he grumbled. "The best

95

beer into England is dark Stout. I must drunk half the country dry of its Stout."

One of the others said, "Them Limeys wasn't so smart. Remember when they was up against it, like, with all Hitler's submarines and all? Well sir, Roosevelt he gave them fifty destroyers to help out, and you know what they did with them? They put 'em in drydock for six months or so changing 'em around so that officer's quarters would be larger and the enlisted men's quarters would be smaller. That's the British for you."

"That's the military mind for you," Old Sam said.

"What's a military mind?"

"The kind where the owner can take off his shirt without unbuttoning the collar."

"Heh, heh, that's pretty good Sam."

Chapter Eleven

Number One was radiating fury as he stalked heavily down the corridors of the Ministry of Internal Affairs. On the surface, his face displayed nothing—which meant nothing. There was simply a raging aura of trouble.

Veljko Gosnjak, posted with one other before the office of Aleksander Kardelj, winced when he saw the Party head approaching. He muttered from the side of his mouth, "Watch out. He's on a rampage. In this mood, he'd as well set you to filling salt shakers in the Siberian mines as . . ."

But Andrei Zorin was now near enough that he might hear, and Veljko Gosnjak cut himself off abruptly and came to even stiffer attention.

Number One ignored them both and pushed on through the door.

Even as his right-hand man looked up from his work, Zorin was growling ominously. "Zeit! Kardelj, I am beginning to suspect that American Hollywood saying is correct. If you have a Hungarian for a friend, you don't need any enemies. Do you know the latest from that brain-wave experiment of yours?"

Kardelj was close enough to the other personally to at least pretend lack of awe. He grinned and said, "You mean young Frol? Sit down, Andrei. A drink?"

The Number Two Party man swiveled slightly and punched out a code on a series of buttons. Almost immediately, an area of approximately one square foot sank down from the upper right-hand corner of his desk to rise again bearing two chilled glasses.

Zorin snorted his anger but took up one of the glasses. "These everlasting gadgets from the West," he growled. "One of these days, this confounded desk of yours will give you an electric shock that will set me to looking for a new assistant." He threw the contents of the glass back over his palate. "If I don't start looking before that time," he said ominously.

Kardelj said, "But what is it that young Frol has done?"

His superior's face resumed its dark expression. He growled, "You know Velimir Crvenkovski, of course."

Kardelj raised scanty eyebrows. "Of course, vice chairman of the Secretariat of Agriculture."

Andrei Zorin had lowered his clumsy bulk into a chair. Now he said heavily, his voice dangerous, "Velimir and I were partisans together. It was I who converted him to the Party, introduced him to the works of Lenin while we squatted in foxholes."

"Of course," the other repeated. "I know the story very well. A good Party man, Comrade Crvenkovski, never

97

failing to vote with you in meetings of the Executive Committee."

"Yes," Zorin growled ominously. "And your precious Frol Krasnaya, your expediter, has removed him from his position as Supreme Commissar of Agriculture in Bosnatia."

Aleksander Kardelj cleared his throat. "I have just been reading the account. It would seem that agricultural production has fallen off considerably in the past five years. Ah . . . Comrade Crvenkovski evidently had brought to his attention that wild life in the countryside, particularly birds, accounted for the loss of hundreds of thousands of tons of cereals annually."

"A well-known fact," Zorin rasped. He finished what remained of his drink, and reached forward to punch out the order for a fresh one. "What has that got to do with this pipsqueak using the confounded powers you invested him with to dismiss one of the best Party men in the Soviet Complex?"

His right-hand man had not failed to note that he was now being given full credit for the expediter idea. He said, still cheerfully, however, "It would seem that Comrade Crvenkovski issued top priority orders to kill off, by whatever means possible, all birds. Shotguns, poison, nets were issued by the tens of thousands to the peasants."

"Well?" his superior said ominously. "Obviously, Velimir was clear minded enough to see the saving in gross production."

"Um-m-m," Kardelj said placatingly. "However, it seems as though the balance of nature calls for the presence of wildlife, and particularly birds. The increase in destructive insects has more than counter-balanced the amount of cereals the birds once consumed. Ah, Zorin," he said with a wry smile, "I sould suggest we find another position for Comrade Crvenkovski."

The secretary-receptionist looked up at long last at the very average-looking young man before him. "Yes?" he said impatiently.

The stranger said, "I would like to see Comrade Broz."

"Surely you must realize that the Commissar is one of the busiest men in Transbalkania, Comrade." There was mocking sneer in the tone. "His time is not at the disposal of every citizen."

The newcomer looked at the petty authority thoughtfully. "Do you so address everyone that enters this office?" he asked mildly.

The other stared at him, flabbergasted. He suddenly banged upon a button on the desk.

When the security guard responded to the summons, he gestured curtly with his head at the newcomer. "Throw this fool out, Petar," he rapped.

Frol Krasnaya shook his head, almost sadly. "No," he said. "Throw *this* man out." He pointed at the secretary-receptionist.

The guard called Petar blinked at each of them in turn.

Frol brought forth his wallet, fidgeted a moment with the contents, then flashed his credentials. "State expediter," he said nervously. "Under direct authority of Comrade Zorin." He looked at the suddenly terrified receptionist. "I don't know what alternative work we can find to fit your talents. However, if I ever again hear of you holding down a position in which you meet the public, I will . . . will . . . see you imprisoned."

The other scurried from the room before Frol thought of more to say.

Frol Krasnaya then looked at the guard for a long moment. He said finally, unhappy still, "What are you needed for around here?"

"Comrade, I am the security guard."

99

"You didn't answer my question." Frol's hands were jittering so he jammed them into his pockets.

Petar was no brain, at best. Finally, however, he came up triumphantly with "Yes, Comrade. I guard Comrade Broz and the others from assassins. I am armed." He proudly displayed the Mikoyan Noiseless which he had holstered under his left shoulder.

Frol said, "Go back to your superior and inform him that I say you are superfluous. No longer are commissars automatically to be guarded. If . . . well, if our people dislike individual commissars sufficiently to wish to assassinate them, maybe they need assassination."

Petar stared at him.

"Oh, get out," Frol said, with attempted sharpness. But then, "What door leads to Comrade Broz's office?"

Petar pointed, then got out. At least he knew how to obey orders, Frol decided. What was there about the police mentality? Were they like that before they became police, and the job sought them out? Or did the job make them all that way?

He pushed his way through the indicated door. The office beyond held but one inhabitant who stood, hands clasped behind his back, while he stared in obvious satisfaction at a wall of charts, maps and graphs.

The average young man looked at some of the lettering on the charts and shook his head. He said, his voice hesitant, "Commissar Broz?"

The other turned, frowning, not recognizing his caller and surprised to find him here without announcement. He said, "Yes, young man?"

Frol presented his credentials again.

Broz had heard of him. He hurried forth a chair, became expansive in manner. A cigar? A drink? A great pleasure to meet the Comrade Expediter. He had heard a great deal about the new experiment initiated by Comrade Zorin and ably assisted by Aleksander Kardelj. Happily, an expediter was not needed in the Transbalkian Steel Complex. It was expanding in such wise as to be the astonishment of the world, both East and West.

"Yes," Frol began glumly, "but——"

Broz was back on his feet and to his wall of charts and graphs. "See here," he beamed expansively. "This curve is steel production. See how it zooms? A veritable Sputnik, eh? Our statistics show that we are rapidly surpassing even the foremost of the Western powers."

Frol Krasnaya said, almost apologetically in veiw of the other's enthusiasm, "That's what I came to discuss with you, Comrade. You see, I've been sitting around, ah, in the local wineshops, talking it over with the younger engineers and the men on the job."

The other frowned at him. "Talking what over?"

"This new policy of yours." Frol's voice was diffident.

"You mean overtaking the steel production of the West, by utilizing *all* methods of production?" The commissar's voice dropped. "I warn you Comrade, the germ of this idea originated with Zorin himself. We are old comrades."

"I'm sure you are," Frol said pessimistically, and suppressing an urge to bite at the skin of his thumb. "However . . . well, I'm not so sure Number One will admit your program originated with him. At least, it hasn't worked out that way in the recent past when something soured."

The other bug-eyed. He whispered, "That approaches cynical treason, Comrade."

The former *Pravda* reporter half nodded, said discouragedly, "You forget. By Comrade Zorin's own orders I . . . I can do no wrong. But so much for that. Now, well, this steel program. I'm afraid it's going to have to be scrapped."

"Scrapped!" the Commissar of the Transbalkanian

Steel Complex stared at his visitor as though the other was rabid. "You fool! Our steel progress is the astonishment of the world! Why, not only are our ultramodern plants, built largely with foreign assistance, working on a twenty-four hour a day basis, but we also have thousands of secondary smelters. Some are so small as to be operated by a handful of comrade citizens; some in backyard establishments by schoolchildren, working smelters of but a few tons monthly capacity."

The newly created State Expediter held up a hand dispiritedly. "I know. I know. Thousands of these backyard smelters exist . . . uh . . . especially in parts of the country where there is neither ore nor fuel available."

The commissar looked at him.

The younger man said, his voice seemingly deprecating his words. "The schoolchildren, taking time off from their studies, of course, bring scrap iron to be smelted. And they bring whatever fuel they can find, often pilfered from railway yards. And the more scrap and fuel they bring, the more praise they get. Unfortunately, the so-called scrap often turns out to be kitchen utensils, farm tools, even, on at least one occasion, some railroad tracks, from a narrow gauge line running up to a lumbering project, not in use that time of the year. Sooner or later, Comrade Broz, the nation is going to have to replace those kitchen utensils and farm tools and all the rest of the scrap that isn't really quite scrap."

The commissar began to protest heatedly, but Frol Krasnaya shook his head and tried to firm his less than dominating voice. "But even that's not the worst of it. Taking citizens away from their real occupations, or studies, and putting them to smelting steel where no ore exists. The worst of it is, so many young engineer friends tell me, that while the steel thus produced might have been a marvel back in the days of the Hittites, it hardly

102

reaches specifications today. Perhaps it might be used ultimately to make simple farm tools such as hoes and rakes; if so, it would make quite an endless circle, because that is largely the source of the so-called steel to begin with—tools, utensils and such. But it hardly seems usable in modern industry."

The commissar had gone pale with anger by now. He put his two fists on his desk and leaned upon them, staring down at his seated visitor. "Comrade," he bit out, "I warn you. Comrade Zorin is enthusiastic about my successes. Beyond that, not only is he an old comrade but my brother-in-law as well."

Frol Krasnaya nodded, unenthusically, and his voice continued to quiver. "So the trained engineers under you, have already warned me. However, Comrade Broz, you are . . . well, no longer Commissar of the Steel Complex. My report has already gone in to Comrades Zorin and Kardelj."

Chapter Twelve

Weigand Patrick, a sheaf of papers held in hand, came happily into the office of the President's personal secretary. He opened his mouth to say something, snapped it shut again.

"Holy smokes!" he blurted. "Who did it!"

"Did what?" Scotty MacDonald said.

"Your blouse. Who tore it?"

"Oh, don't be silly. This is the latest thing. The Cretan Revival."

"Cretan Revival! Wasn't that Agnes Sorel Revival bad

enough? Now both of them are sticking out." He added, suspiciously, "And you've put lipstick or something on the tips."

"I have not."

"You have so. You're a shameless hussy. Which reminds me. When are we going to finally cosummate this seduction?"

Scotty snorted. "The way you operate, I'm thinking of getting somebody else to do the job."

He looked at her incredulously. "You can't do that."

"Why not?"

"Because I owe it to you to be first. I'm the most incomparable lover in the world."

"Ha!"

He leaned over her desk earnestly. "But I am. I'm half German, half Irish, and half French and everybody knows that makes the most competent lover possible."

"That makes three halves," she muttered sarcastically, "and that's not even counting half-assed."

"What?"

"Nothing," she yawned. "What makes you such an incomparable lover? What do you do that anybody else doesn't?"

He looked around the room, as though checking that no one else might hear, then bent nearer and whispered, "I kiss a woman's navel."

She stared at him, "Kiss a woman's navel? What's so wonderful about that?"

"Yes, but, *from inside?*"

"Oh, shut up, you fool. How's it going?"

"So far, so good. We had to move the whole shebang into the Green Room, so we could crowd all the news boys in."

She looked at him suspiciously. "Something's going on here I don't know about. What's the point in having the press present at a Fireside Chat? It's live. They could get it on their Tri-Di sets."

Weigand Patrick grinned slyly. "I want them present. Real eye witnesses. So nobody can say later it was a Tri-Di rigged optical illusion. I wonder what happened to that kid from *Pravda,* Frol Krasnaya. I especially wanted *Pravda* to be there."

"Another thing. What happened to Fred Moriarty? He hasn't been around for a week."

Weigand put his forefinger to the side of his nose in a burlesque of the presidential gesture of slyness and winked at her. "He's all right. He'll probably be back after the elections are over. He's taken a trip south."

"Something's going on here, WeeWee Patrick, that I don't think I like. What's Old Chucklehead all done up in that conservative suit for? He looks like a preacher. Usually, he tends toward Hawaiian shirts and slacks a juvenile delinquent would consider far out."

"Don't call him that!" Weigand said. "And stop calling me WeeWee. You'll see. After this broadcast, this Administration will have a prestige that'll carry it on for the next half dozen campaigns. I'm thinking of running him at least four times, like Roosevelt."

"That can't be done, any more."

"That's what you think, honey. After tonight, we're going to have Congress sitting in our hand."

"Well, watch out what they do in your palm," Scotty snorted.

Weigand looked at his watch. "I'll have to get on in there. The Sachem is scheduled on in ten minutes. I want to make some preliminary remarks, especially to that bastard Harrison from *Newsweek* who's been writing those Anti-Adams columns."

He looked down at her severely, "How about tonight. Let's have a definite answer. What do you say?"

Scotty said sarcastically, "As Benjamin Franklin put it, Masturbation is its own reward."

He glared at her for a moment then said, "Listen, that reminds me of something. That song and dance you were giving me the other night about Ponce DeLeon's pants. How they fell in the Fountain of Youth. What finally happened?"

"What do you think happened? He became the biggest foul-up in the history of seduction. Finally, the Indians killed him."

"Hmmm. The Indian *men* or the Indian *women?*"

She snorted at him. "Guess."

Weigand Patrick staggered back into Scotty's room, his face ashen.

Scotty MacDonald, who was still staring in fascination at the Tri-Di box, in the corner of her office, turned to him.

"Holy smokes," he muttered.

"What in the world happened, there?"

"Holy smokes," he protested.

She said, "There was something funny in the transmission. It was like a comedy effect. Some kind of static."

He groaned and sank into a chair, and put his head in his hands.

"The halo," he said. "The damned halo was on wrong."

"Halo?" Scotty said. "You mean that thing like a ferris wheel, or a fireworks pinwheel, or whatever it looked like?"

"It was supposed to be horizontal," he moaned loudly. "*Horizontal* not vertical."

"Old Chucklehead sure looked funny," Scotty said sympathetically.

Polly Adams wandered in from the presidential study, her expression vaguely troubled.

106

She said, "Weigand, I think Horace was looking for you."

He groaned aloud.

The First Lady said vacantly, "I'm going to have to tell William to stop putting so little vermouth in the Martinis—or something." She brightened slightly. "Perhaps I should see my oculist."

Weigand moaned.

Polly Adams said, "Perhaps I'll just tell him to put *less* vermouth in." She wandered out again.

Scotty looked after her thoughtfully. She said, "I'm going to have to suggest to Hilda that Polly be sent back to that beauty-and-health diet spot in Colorado, to get dried out again."

Weigand groaned and said, "Scotty, get me Edgar, will you?"

"Edgar?"

"On the phone screen. Fred Moriarty's coming back sooner than I thought."

Chapter Thirteen

The conference table was crowded, the room thick with cigar smoke, Walthers was trotting back and forth to the bar, refreshing glasses.

A large tweedy type, a huge bent-stem pipe in the side of his mouth, was saying, "We'll have to issue these on various price levels. Make it a status symbol, the amount you've blown on your Pilgrimage of Jeanne d'Arc game."

Somebody interrupted. "I don't like using them fancy foreign names. What's the matter with using her right name, Joan of Arc?"

Les Frankle, sitting to one side, said unhappily, "The only record we have of her signature, she signed her name *Jeanette*." He hadn't pitched his voice high enough to be heard.

A fat man in the gaudy clothing of the Coast, puffed cheeks and rumbled in agreement. "Ed's right. Using, like, French words and all that'd just antagonize folks back in the boondocks. Make her sound too high falutin. Let's call her Joan of Arc."

The tweedy type closed his eyes momentarily, in mute protest but said, "Why don't we do this? On the game sets peddling for only ten dollars, we'll call it the Joan of Arc Pilgrimage. But on the sets retailing for twenty-five and up, we'll use the Jeanne d'Arc name. The people with boodle enough left to invest that amount in a game will get an added status symbol in the French."

The Professor, at table's end, had been beaming benignly at the discussion. Now he put in, "Gentlemen, we must remember in concocting this game to strike the correct intellectual level. We do not wish something as double-domed as *Scrabble*, that would eliminate too many potential customers. Nor anything as simple as *Parchesi*, that is for children and this is an adult fad."

Jimmy Leath, as silent thus far as Les Frankle, grumbled, "And nothing as crass as *Monopoly*. Remember, Joan is a saint. Very high moral tone, that sort of thing."

The tweedy type took his pipe from his mouth and said, "We have all that in mind. However, the Pilgrimage is strictly for adults, but Joan is taking on with the kids too."

"Sure is," someone else muttered. We flubbed on the mother and daughter Joan of Arc clothes sets. Way behind on orders."

"I suggest we bring out a simplified form of the game for children," the tweedy type said.

"For children and our simpler adults," Les Frankle said unhappily.

"Very well, By George," the Professor said. "So it is with the Pilgrimage game. The Maid is really catching on."

"What's this *the Maid* stuff?" the fat man from California said. "You're talking about Joan, aren't you?"

Les Frankle spoke up, loud enough to be heard this time. "Well, women belonging to the Jeanne d'Arc Clubs have taken to calling her The Maid of Orleans. Irene says it's an instinctive reaction toward the virgin principle which dominates——"

"Who's the hell's Irene?" the tweedy type wanted to know.

Les Frankle looked at him. "Irene's my wife," he said. "Doctor Irene Frankle." He shifted uncomfortably. "She's also national president of the Jeanne d'Arc Clubs."

"*She is?*" the Professor blurted. "No wonder we were not able to get a percentage of the dues from those clubs."

Somebody else said, "We worked that out two weeks ago. It'd be too obvious if our syndicate tried to get in on spontaneously organized clubs. Too bad, though, they've swept the nation."

The Professor looked at Les accusingly. "You failed to inform me of Irene's membership, not to speak of her presidency, By Ceorge."

"Well," Les said doggedly, "you know how Irene is, sir. She's got a regular phobia about joining all these women's do-gooder outfits and all. She believes that organizations like this syndicate . . ." he flushed and nodded around unhappily to the table as a whole ". . . are, well, destroying the nation."

The tweedy type blurted, "Just what do you mean by that, young man!"

Les looked at him unhappily. "Well, that's what Irene says, sir. Such organizations as Doolittle Research, the other MR outfits and the ad agencies manipulate human motivations and desires and develop a need for products with which the public has previously been unfamiliar, perhaps even undesirous of purchasing. She thinks that's ultimately turning the country into a nation of idiots, besides wasting natural resources."

The fat man was on his feet. "See here! I didn't come to this conference to be insulted." He glared at Professor Doolittle. "Who is this young ass, Professor?"

Doolittle came to his own feet, and lifted his chubby paws placatingly. "Gentlemen, gentlemen, please." He smiled benignly at Les Frankle, then returned to his confreres seated at the table.

"You members of the Oedipus Group think tank are, ah, pragmatic businessmen. My lad, Les, here, is a high trained double—that is, psychologist from one of the nation's very top universities. His field is mass behavior, gentlemen, and, By George, he knows it. In discussing mass behavior, gentlemen, you draw on Durkheim in sociology, Korzbski in semantics, Whitehead in symbolic logic—I could go on. How many of you are acquainted with the works of these, ah, to use the idiom, crystal gazers? Gentlemen, if the past couple of decades has taught the businessman anything, it is that we need more whiskers—ah, that is, professors—not fewer. My lads here, Lester and James, are top men in their fields, as you are in yours. We need them." He chuckled. "And they need the money we pay them."

He said indulgently, "And now shall we have a report from our publisher? Undoubtedly, you gentlemen are already aware that our biography of Joan is still at the top of the non-fiction best sellers, and two of our novels on

her are pushing second and fourth places. But now, this
series of children's books. . . ."

Chapter Fourteen

The knock came at the door in the middle of the night,
as Aleksander Kardelj had always thought it would.

From those early days of his party career, when his
ambitions had sent him climbing, pushing, tripping up
others, on his way to the top, he had expected it eventually.

Oh, his had been a different approach, on the surface,
an easygoing, gentler approach than one usually connected with members of the Secretariat of the Executive
Committee of the Party, but it made very little difference
in the very long view. When one fell from the heights,
he fell just as hard, whether or not he was noted for
his sympathetic easy humor.

The fact was, Aleksander Kardelj was not asleep when
the fist pounded at his door shortly after midnight. He
had but recently turned off, with a shaking hand, the
phone screen, after a less than pleasant conversation
with Andrei Zorin.

For the past ten years, Kardelj had been able to pla-
cate Zorin, even though Number One be at the peak of
a surly rage, rages which seemed to be coming with in-
creasing frequency of late. As the socio-economic system
of the People's Democratic Dictatorship became increasingly complicated, as industrialization with its modern
automation mushroomed in a geometric progression, the
comparative simplicity of governing was strictly of yes-

teryear. Industrialization calls for a highly educated element of scientists and technicians, nor does it stop there. One of sub-mentality can operate a shovel in a field, or even do a simple operation on an endless assembly line in a factory, but practically all workers must be highly skilled workers in the age of automation, and there is little room for the illiterate. The populace of the People's Dictatorship was no longer a dumb, driven herd, and their problems were no longer simple ones.

Yes, Number One was increasingly subject to his rages these days.It was Aleksander Kardelj's belief that Zorin was finding himself out of his depth. And he who is confused, be he ditchdigger or dictator, is a man emotionally upset.

Andrei Zorin's face had come onto the phone screen already enraged. He had snapped to his right-hand man, "Kardelj! Do you realize what the . . . that idiot of yours has been up to now?"

Inwardly, Kardelj had winced. His superior had been mountingly difficult of late, and particularly these past few days. He said now, cajolingly, "Andrei, I——"

"Don't call me Andrei, Kardelj! And please preserve me from your sickening attempts to fawn, in view of your treacherous recommendations of recent months."

Kardelj had never seen him this furious. He said placatingly, "Comrade Zorin, I had already come to the conclusion that I should consult you on the desirability of revoking this young troublemaker's credentials and removing him from the——"

"I am not interested in what you were *going* to do, Kardelj. I am already in the process of ending this traitor's activities. I should have known, when you revealed he was the son of Alex Krasnaya, that he was an enemy of the State, deep within."

Kardelj had enough courage left to say, "Comrade, it

112

would seem to me that young Krasnaya is a tanglefoot, but not a conscious traitor. I——"

"Don't call me comrade, Kardelj!" Number One roared. "I know your inner motivation. The reason you brought this Trotskyite wrecker to his position of ridiculous power. The two of your are in conspiracy to undermine my authority. I've heard about you Hungarians. The only people in the world that can go into a revolving door behind you and come out first! This will be brought before the Secretariat of the Executive Committee, Kardelj. You've gone too far, this time!"

Aleksander Kardelj had his shortcomings but he was no coward. He said, wryly, "Very well, sir. But would you tell me what Frol has done now? My office has had no report on him for some time."

"What has he done! You fool, you traitorous fool, have you kept no record at all? He has been in the Kirghiz area where my virgin lands program has been in full swing."

Kardelj cleared his throat at this point.

Zorin continued roaring. "The past three years, admittedly, the weather has been such, the confounded rains failing to arrive on schedule, that we have had our troubles. But this fool! This blundering traitorous idiot!"

"What has he done?" Kardelj asked, intrigued in spite of his position of danger.

"For all practical purposes he's ordered the whole program reversed. Something about a sandbowl developing, whatever that is supposed to mean. Something about introducing contour plowing, whatever nonsense that is. And even reforestating some areas. Some nonsense about watersheds. He evidently has blinded and misled the very men I had in charge. They are supporting him, openly."

Zorin, Kardelj knew, had been a miner as a youth,

with no experience whatsoever on the soil. However, the virgin lands project had been his pet. He envisioned hundreds upon thousands of square miles of maize, corn, as the Americans called it. This in turn would feed vast herds of cattle and swine so that ultimately the Soviet Complex would have the highest meat consumption in the world.

Number One was raging on. Something about a conspiracy on the part of those who surrounded him. A conspiracy to overthrow him, Andrei Zorin, and betray the revolution to the Western powers, but he, Andrei Zorin, had been through this sort of plot before. He, Andrei Zorin, knew the answers to such situations.

Aleksander Kardelj grinned wryly, and reached to flick off the screen. He twisted a cigarette into the small pipelike holder, lit it and waited for the inevitable.

It was shortly after that the knock came on his door.

Chapter Fifteen

Marv and Phoebe Sellers sat at the kitchen table of their house at 4011 Camino de Palmas, Tucson, Arizona.

Marv looked around at their packed belongings bitterly.

"Dave oughta be here with his truck, pretty soon," he said. "You sure your folks don't mind us moving in with them?"

Phoebe shrugged. "I suppose they mind, Marv. But what can they do? It's happening all around town; people move in with each other to save rent. How long do you think it'll take to sell the house?"

"I don't know, Phoebe. Houses ain't moving any too good

these days. Practically nothing's moving that I can see except maybe these crazy Joan of Arc fad things. You'd think folks would have more on their mind than running around wearing little swords during times like these."

"Keeps their minds offen their troubles, I guess," Phoebe said placidly. "Can't begrudge them that." She looked at him. "What do you think we'll get for the house, Marv?"

"Not very much, we ain't got much equity into it. Where's Old Sam?"

"He's in the next room, messing around in some of that old junk he had stored away in a trunk in the garage. What're we gonna do, Marv?"

He shrugged his depression. "I don't know, Phebe. Just go on relief like everybody else, I guess. What else?"

"I heard tell the city was cutting back on relief. They run out of money. They ain't even paying the teachers and the garbage men any more. It's getting to be a chore, burying the garbage out in the yard though precious little garbage we got these days, anyways. We eat it."

Old Sam came in chortling.

"What've you got there, fer crissake, Gramps?" Marv said disinterestedly.

"You'll see," the oldster chuckled. He had a big piece of cardboard in one hand, a box of crayons in the other. He laid the cardboard out on the table, selected a crayon and began to color in a big black zero.

Marv, frowning, got up and looked over his shoulder. He read, slowly, *Unemployed. Please Buy an Apple. 50¢.*

Old Sam chortled again. "You young people never listen to me when I tell you about the old days. You'll see. I'll make us some pocket money."

Marv said accusingly, "That sign used to read 5¢. How come you've upped it to 50¢?"

"Inflation," Old Sam said cryptically. "Found this here sign in the bottom of my trunk. Kind of forgot about it. You stand out on the street corner with a box of apples and this sign. Mint money."

"I'll bet, Gramps," Marv muttered.

Chapter Sixteen

The President was slumped in his chair at his brain trust round table, after still another disastrous conference. The only ones left were Fred Moriarty, and Weigand Patrick.

"Double-domes," Horace Adams said in complaint. "Craminently. First one wants to cut back government expenditures by firing half the bureaucracy. That puts near ten more million people on unemployment. Another one wants to bring up prices, like Roosevelt did, by plowing under cotton, that sort of thing. But they want to go him one better. This depression is *really* big. This time, they want to pour petroleum back into the wells, and shovel coal back into the mines."

Weigand Patrick and Fred Moriarty held their peace.

The President mumbled, "But that one from Princeton's right. We've got to save money some way. Fort Knox is practically empty."

His face brightened. "There's one thing, Weigand, get in touch with the National Aeronautics and Space Council to discontinue the Space program. Can't afford to be shooting all that crap up into the sky. If they won't allow me to liberate Mozambique and contain Finland, I don't see how we can afford to colonize the moon."

Weigand blinked. "Yes, Mr. President," he said. "The

116

moon base. How about the men we already have up there?"

"How many of them are there?"

"Eight altogether," Moriarty supplied.

"How much will it cost to bring them back?"

Moriarty looked vague. He had a wonderful tan these days, from his recent subjection to the Floridian sun; however, from time to time, his glances at Weigand Patrick were less than comradely.

Weigand clicked his pipe stem against his teeth unhappily. "I'd estimate about a billion dollars, Chief."

The President scratched himself. "This heavy underwear Polly has me in sure itches. You'd think that cutting down on the burning of oil would be something unnecessary in the White House."

Weigand lit his pipe. "Sets an example, sir," he said. "Johnson used to turn out the lights."

Horace Adams looked at him balefully. "Whatever you're smoking in that thing, smells like what I put on my strawberries."

"Strawberries?" Moriarty said blankly. "I put sugar and cream on mine."

The President snorted, "In the garden, not in the plate."

Weigand sighed and put his corncob back in his pocket.

The President thought about the space colonists on the moon for a long moment, sighed at another of his projects going down the drain and grunted. "Leave them there. They're expendable. Raise a big monument to them. It'll be cheaper. I'll speak at its dedication. Very sentimental."

Weigand winced but held his peace.

Horace Adams snorted, "What do you think about this reopening relationships with Cuba?"

"Well, it has its points, sir," Moriarty said. "Keep the unemployed a bit more tranquil. Back when times were booming, everybody was in a hurry and smoked cigarettes. Now that everybody's sitting around, watching Tri-Di, they've got time for a long smoke. Some people are pretty serious about that new slogan: What this country needs is a good dollar cigar—what with inflation."

The President grunted. "Talking about slogans, what do you think about the one proposed by Professor Markham to keep up morale? Prosperity Is Just Around the Corner."

Weigand said thoughtfully, "I think I've heard that somewhere before. My instinct is to believe it won't be well received by the older generations."

The President glared at him. "Confound it, Weigand, why don't *you* come up with something? You're supposed to be my whizz-bang advisor."

Weigand Patrick stirred in his chair, automatically he reached for his corncob, remembered and put it back. He said slowly, "To tell the truth, Mr. President, I think I have the germ of an idea."

"Well, in the name of Moses, what is it? I've been listening to drivel for the past four hours, a little more can't hurt."

Patrick nodded and absently reached for pipe and tobacco pouch still once again.

"Sir, remember when I was telling you how a depression got started? The slow start, and then the snowball effect? Just like boom begets boom, bust begets bust?"

"How could I forget, damn it? It was the first time I ever heard of a depression."

"Yes, sir. Well, it occurred to me that *somewhere* this depression had to start. Some single place in the country. Some single action." He paused for effect.

118

The President was staring at him, as was Fred Moriarty. a glimmering of hope far behind their eyes.

"So?" Horace Adams rasped.

Weigand shrugged his lazy shrug, and lit the corncob. "So, suppose we trace it down. Suppose we get to this root of the evil. This starting point."

The President still stared. His voice was slightly hoarse.

"Then what do we do?"

Weigand Patrick replaced the tobacco pouch in his right pocket, the matches in his left. He blew smoke from his nostrils.

"We play it by ear," he said.

Later, on his way back to his own office in the Right Wing, Weigand Patrick passed through Scotty's room.

She said, "Well, what did Old Chucklehead come up with this time? Another big plan to dam up the Missouri River and have it flow backward over the Rocky Mountains?"

"Nothing special," Weigand told her.

She made a face. "Listen, do you think we ought to shoot him?"

"Shoot him!" he blurted. "Holy smokes!"

She said, "Well? Here the country's in the biggest emergency in its history, and we've got the biggest chucklehead in the executive mansion, ever, and that's saying a lot when you consider some of the past ones. Talk about the bland leading the bland, ha!"

He said reasonably, "It doesn't do any good. It's been tried and you always wind up with somebody worse than the one you shot."

Scotty said worriedly, "We've got to do something. Did you catch that Tri-Di speech from the Senate, that old queen Smogborne?"

119

"What'd he have to say?"

"Legalization of homosexuality between consenting males. Like the British. He claims that the number of homos that would shack up together would start a boom in housing, and house furniture."

Weigand thought about it. "You know, come to think of it, in Hollywood alone. . . ." He shook his head in marvel. "I'd like a blow by blow description of the first night in that town if they legalized homosexuality."

Scotty snorted. "I wonder if he includes Lesbians. The way my sex life is going, I might consider——"

"Hey! None of that now. Listen, as soon as I get this new project under way——"

"Ha!" Scotty snorted. "My juices are already beginning to dry up, waiting for you. I'm an old maid and don't know it. Look, I hate to bring this up again, but why don't you marry me?"

"Marry you?" Weigand said plaintively. "I keep telling you, I'm a great lover, but I'd be a lousy husband. I'm so improvident, I can go into a cold shower and come out three dollars poorer."

Chapter Seventeen

"Doublets and hose?" Warren Dempsey Witherson said blankly. "Pseudo-mail? What in the hell is pseudo-mail?" He pushed his pince-nez glasses back onto the bridge of his nose with his left forefinger and stared at Jimmy Leath.

"Pseudo-mail is a new type of sweater we've brought out for men. It's practically the only thing selling now in sweaters. The industry is in a tizzy."

Witherson was still blank. "But what is it?"

"Pseudo-mail is a form of weave that makes the sweater look like mail." Neither of the two older men had yet reacted, so he grunted and added, "Mail was the predominant type of armor used in the days of Jeanne d'Arc."

"Oh," Warren Dempsey Witherson beamed. "And we're to publicize it, eh? My boy, from what you say, it doesn't need much publicizing."

"No sir. It seems to have swept the country, whether men want it or not. Our research shows that women, ultimately, buy, or influence to the decisive point, the buying of approximately eighty-five percent of male clothing."

"Well, how about these tin shirts the women are wearing?"

Jimmy ran a hand back through his hair in irritation. "Well, that's another thing. We didn't start that. It was spontaneous and other manufacturers got in on it before we could dominate the field."

"What's this, By George?" the Professor interjected, indignantly. He had been sitting quietly until now.

"Corselets," Jimmy Leath growled. "They're making them largely out of aluminum, but sometimes the lighter steel alloys. God knows, you've seen enough of the Joan of Arc illustrations we've put on the calendars and such. The popular idea is that in combat she wore a corselet. It's body armor, the breast plate and the back piece together."

Witherson was staring at him. "You mean, some grifter not on our team has managed to con the marks into wearing——"

The Professor interrupted indulgently. "What the good doctor is saying, James, is that it seems unlikely that a modern, style-conscious woman would be seen in public in such a contraption."

"I don't know, sir," Jimmy said. "The way they've done them up, they look cute. Besides, it wasn't until just lately they wore them in public, especially for evening wear. At first, it was just at their club meetings. You know, something like the Shriners in their Arab outfits, or the American Legion, or the Boy Scouts."

"Club meetings, eh?" the Professor said thoughtfully. He flicked his hand over an eye-button on his desk and said into empty air, "Walthers, send in Mr. Frankle."

While they waited, he said to Jimmy. "What's this about doublets and hose?"

Jimmy snorted. "That's another one that Les seemed to underestimate in his depth research. He figured there'd be a small market for 15th Century costume for masquerades. What we didn't figure on is the pressure these women seem to be able to put to bear once they get on the Joan of Arc kick. That and the fact that men haven't had any really basic change in their clothes since the Civil War. We're still wearing the same basic coats, vests and long trousered pants Lincoln did."

Witherson hacked thoughtfully a few times and then said, "I'll put the boys to work on it. Maybe we can get President Adams to give his next press conference in this new outfit. Doublet and hose, eh? I'll bring it up at the next brain trust meeting."

. Jimmy shuddered but said, "It's no use our trying to pick it up now. Every men's clothing manufacturer in the country is switching. In a week or so, you'll be out of style wearing a suit."

Les Frankle, worried of expression, came in and said, "Yes, sir."

Doolittle picked up a report from his desk. "You wouldn't know anything about this complaint from the

French vintner concern that handles the Jeanne d'Arc Lorraine wines, the Saint Joan Rheims champagne and Joan of Arc Three Star Cognac?"

"Well, no sir," Les said. "Not much. I've been looking into this gold and diamond charm bracelet project with the designers from Tiff——"

The Professor interrupted easily. "Before I forget, you had better drop that charm with Joan being burnt at the stake. The one with the chip rubies for fire. A bit on the bad taste side, lad. By George, this fad must be kept on the highest moral level. Is that not so, Doctor?"

Doctor Witherson cleared his throat. "Our only motivation," he beamed. "That and aiding our great President to combat the depression."

"Now, these riots in Kansas by the members of the Jeanne d'Arc Clubs. This dashing into bars and liquor stores, breaking up bottles with those swords of theirs. Really, By George, what is up?"

"Well, sir, from what Irene says, the newspapers have the wrong idea. It's not a Carrie Nation sort of thing at all."

"Irene!" the Professor blurted.

"Who's Carrie Nation?" Jimmy Leath said.

Les said, "A feminist back in the Victorian period. She was a temperance leader. Used to go into saloons with a hatchet and break up the place."

"You mean," the Professor demanded, "That these Kansas riots aren't of a temperance nature?"

Les said uncomfortably, "Well, no sir. Not according to Irene. She says they're a spontaneous rebellion against those French wine companies using the Jeanne d'Arc name. It seems as though United Consumers reported on the Jeanne d'Arc wines and cognacs and found them unacceptable buys. Uh . . . I believe dishwater was the descriptive term."

"United Consumers!" the Professor blurted. "That consortium of subversives."

"Well, yes sir," Les said, flushing. "It seems as though the clubs have a ruling that all members have to subscribe to the montly United Consumers reports. Uh . . . Irene kind of rammed that requirement through."

Witherson was indignant. "This should be actionable. How could those Frog . . . ah, that is, French vintners possibly turn out a first grade product when you consider the score we rake off before——"

"Ah, Doctor," the Professor said placatingly. "We'll consider the matter in executive council, later."

Les said, "I think we're going to have trouble on that sports car deal too. That air cushion model that looks vaguely like an armored horse, and has the head of the Maid on . . ."

"Trouble?" Witherson bleated. "Why, the take we were to get on that——"

"Doctor, Doctor," the Professor said. He turned a pompous eye on Les Frankle. "I suppose you have further inside information from Irene?"

"Well, in a way. She mentioned, kind of in passing, at dinner last night, that the clubs were going to boycott the car. Too big and heavy for average use, too expensive to run, and most likely the style will be obsolete within a year. Besides that, she says half the cost went into its silly decorations. According to Irene, it's time for the women of the country to put their feet down in regard to the kind of cars we're buying."

The Professor's eyes went to Jimmy Leath. "Well, James, my lad, do you have any ideas? Both the French wine deal and the line-up with the Saint Joan sports car were sizeable amounts."

Jimmy grunted sourly. He said, "We're putting out three different Jeanne d'Arc magazines now, one for the upper lowers, one for the lower middles and one for the quality market. We might suggest to the concerns involved that they step up their advertising and at the same time we'll do some free articles pushing their products."

The Professor pursed plump lips, "Now, James, we begin to get somewhere."

Les was shaking his head, unhappily. "Club members have been infiltrating the magazine staffs, according to Irene. It seems that it can't be helped because nobody else is in a position to know what the readers want. Nobody else is up enough on the Maid and her principles."

"Her what?" Witherson said blankly, pushing his glasses back.

"Her beliefs," Les said earnestly. "What she really stood for. Anyway, club members are largely editing the three magazines the syndicate launched and beginning next week they're not going to take any ads that aren't absolutely accurate in describing the product advertised. If Jeann d'Arc wine tastes like dishwater, they just won't accept the ad." He added, lamely, "At least, that's what Irene said."

"Lester," the Professor said, his voice lacking its usual beneficient quality. "Irene seems to have taken an inordinate interest in the affairs of the Oedipus Group."

"Oh, no, sir," Les Frankle said hurriedly. "It's not that. You see, Professor Doolittle, Irene has had this interest in Joan, the Maid of Orleans, ever since she was a child. It's a regular phobia with her."

It was a full Oedipus Group conference again. The room smoke filled again. Walthers trotting about with drinks again. Professor Doolittle presiding again, his youthful staff to one side, Doctor Warren Dempsey Witherson to the other.

125

The Professor kept his own report until the last, beaming benevolently at his colleagues as they reported on Tri-Di movies and television, on radio programs and song records and tapes, on games for both adults and children, on textile sales, on swords, armor and the new medieval revival styles, on tours to France and publishing house sales of biographies, novels and comic books.

The Professor beamed through it all. Save for minor upsets, and intrusions of Johnnies-come-lately who were continually climbing aboard the Joan of Arc bandwagon, the reports were upbeat in nature.

When at last he came to his own feet, the hush was pronounced. It was not like the Professor to have kept himself from the limelight for so long.

The Professor dry washed his hands, jovially.

"Well, gentlemen, we now come to the jackpot, By George. Until now, all has been peanuts, as idiom would have it."

"Five million net from our Jeanne d'Arc Pilgrimage game isn't exactly peanuts," the tweedy type muttered. He was in Donegals today, a curved Peterson shell briar in his mouth.

"Peanuts," the Professor cackled indulgently. "Gentlemen, what is the biggest single industry in this great and glorious nation of ours?"

"Automobiles," somebody growled. "We already got into that flop of a sports air-cushion car up in Detroit."

"A.T. and T." the fat man from California said. Of them all, he looked the most ridiculous in doublet and hose. "The biggest single company is Telephone."

The Professor waggled a happy finger at him. "The biggest company, perhaps, but not the biggest industry, By George. Gentlemen, the biggest industry in this great nation of ours is government. It hires more people, it

126

spends more money, than any other six groups of industries combined."

Witherson blinked at him. "You mean we're going to take over the government, Professor?" He hacked his throat clear, pushed his pince-nez glasses back on the bridge of his nose, nervously.

The Professor eyed him benignly. "Only in a manner of speaking, my dear Doctor."

He turned his eyes back to the others. "Gentlemen, I have been approached by representatives of both political parties. Both realize the position we occupy. Gentlemen, the way matters are shaping up, the elections this fall could be the nearest thing to a tie our glorious country has seen for many a decade. Yes, By George," he beamed, "if we should stand idly by and not, ah, perform our duty, the election could well be a tie."

Warren Dempsey Witherson cleared his throat again. "Our duty?"

The Professor's voice was gentle. "The only term, my dear Doctor. To arrive at a decision on just whom to support, and then, ah, throw the full resources of the Joan of Arc movement into the blanace."

The tweedy type said, "What decision? Who offered the most?"

"We are still dickering," the Professor told him.

Jimmy Leath growled, "Sir, are we going to be able to deliver the vote of the Joan of Arc fans? That's the question."

The Professor turned on him, kindly. "James, my lad, that is where our think tank comes in. In putting over this fad of ours, and enriching ourselves in the process, we have also built up the strongest team in the fields of motivational research, advertising, psychology applied to sales research, mass behaviorism and related subjects that this great nation has ever seen. By George, it is most inspiring."

He waxed eloquent, flourishing a fat, freckled paw in emphasis. "Gentlemen, some fifty percent of the women voters of America are presently influenced by the Joan of Arc fad. Of these, at least thirty millions are deeply involved. We have the next election in the palm of our collective hand. We could even re-elect Horace Adams, which ordinarily would seem an impossibility."

The fat man from California was beginning to get the message. "Why, why . . . it's the biggest thing since . . . since. . . ."

"Since Didius bought the Roman Empire," Jimmy Leath murmured, massaging his stomach.

They broke into excited jabbering.

The tweedy type was saying thoughtfully. "We'll have to line up the star of our original Tri-Di movie. Lots of the Joan fans identify her face with the original Joan. Then we'll have to line up the actors on TV and radio who portray Joan. Then we'll have to swing our magazines, even the comic books, over to our candidate."

"Who's that?" somebody said stupidly.

"Who knows, so far?" Witherson said reasonably. "You heard the Professor, the dickering is still going on."

"We'll really have to probe this in depth," Jimmy was muttering, intrigued. "Cover the country like smog. Find out what all these dizzy dames want our candidate to consider the issues of the day, besides the depression, of course. Control the widest blanket of polls, do the greatest number of depth interviews, ever seen. Given the Joan fans to begin with, as a lever, we can take this country like Grant. . . ."

The Professor was beaming still. "Gentlemen," he said. "I can assure you, By George, that we are not about to sell our services for small return. When all the smoke has cleared, we here in this room will be in the catbird seat."

Les Frankle said unhappily, "Irene isn't going to like this."

Chapter Eighteen

Weigand Patrick took in the long rows of computers, the clacking sorters and tabulators, the collators and key punches.

He shook his head and said, "Let's get out of this noise."

The other led him to an office. The door that closed behind them was soundproofed.

"Holy Smokes," Weigand said, "how do you do any thinking in that?"

"We don't have to do any thinking," Rod Watson told him. "The machines do the thinking."

Weigand Patrick looked at him, even while fumbling in his doublet pocket for his pipe. "Damn these fancy clothes," he muttered.

Watson said, "And after they've done their thinking, we bring the results into offices like this and think about what they thought about."

"Very funny," Weigand said. "I'll tell the President how this department produces jollies."

Rod Watson blanched.

Weigand said, "Okay, okay, I won't really. He's on a retrenchment binge these days. Bring down expenses. Let go some of the millions of governmental employees that've been pyramiding ever since Hoover. He put the whole Navy in mothballs. Economy is economy, I suppose, but if you ask me firing the Air Force is kind of gelding the lily."

"Fired the Air Force?" Watson said unbelievingly.

"That's right. He figures, what do you need an Air Force for with all the missiles we've got? At any rate, how far did you get today?"

Rod Watson walked around to the other side of his desk, sat down and selected a report. "Detroit," he said, "According to the computors, the beginning of the big crackup was when Detroit cut back production and laid off about a hundred thousand men. That's when it really started snowballing."

Patrick was lighting his pipe. He shook his head wear-

"No," he said. "You don't understand what I want from you, Watson. That wasn't when it started snowballing. By that time, the avalanche was well under way."

Watson was scowling at him.

Weigand Patrick pointed with his pipe stem at the second button on the other's fancy doublet. "*Why* did Detroit cut back?"

Watson blinked. "Why? Why, isn't that obvious? The new model cars weren't selling."

"Why? Take it further back."

Rod Watson looked distressed. "See here, Mr. Patrick, the Bureau of Statistics isn't omniscient."

Weigand Patrick puffed gently on his corncob. "Then it better get that way. Don't forget the Air Force, Rod, old man."

Watson closed his eyes in anguish. "Just what is it you want, Mr. Patrick?"

"Go further back," Weigand Patrick waved vaguely in the direction of the machine rooms. "Somewhere in all that accumulated data in there, you can find the *beginning* of it all. The first single grain of sand that started down the mountainside, joggling other grains, then pebbles, then rocks, until finally the avalanche was on us."

Watson groaned.

Chapter Nineteen

Andrei Zorin sat at his desk in the Ministry of Internal Affairs, a heavy military revolver close to his right hand, a half empty liter of vodka and a water tumbler, to his ' left. Red of eye, he pored over endless reports from his agents, occasionally taking time out to growl a command into his desk mike. As tired as he was, from the long sleepless hours he was putting in, Number One was in his element. As he had told the incompetent, Kardelj, he had been through this thing before. It was no mistake that he was Number One.

He snapped into the mike, "Give me Lazar Jovanovic." And then, when the police head's shaven poll appeared in the screen of the phone screen, "Comrade, I am giving you one last chance. Produce this traitor, Frol Krasnaya, within the next twenty-four hours, or answer to me." He glared at the other, whose face had tightened in fear. "I begin to doubt the sincerity of your efforts in this, Comrade Jovanovic."

He flicked off the instrument, then glowered at it for a full minute. If Jovanovic couldn't locate Krasnaya, he'd find someone who could. It was maddening that the pipsqueak had seemingly disappeared. To this point, seeking him had progressed in secret. There had been too much favorable publicity churned out in the early days of the expediter scheme to reverse matters to the point of having a public hue and cry.

131

The gentle summons of his phone screen tinkled, and he flicked it on with a rough brush of his hand.

And there was the youthful face of Frol Krasnaya, currently being sought high and low by the full strength of the Internal Affairs Secretariat. Youthful, yes, but even as he stared his astonishment, Andrei Zorin could see that the past months had wrought their changes on the other's face. It was more mature, bore more of strain and weariness.

Before Zorin found his voice, Frol Krasnaya said diffidently, "I . . . I understand you've been, well . . . looking for me, sir."

"Looking for you!" the Party head bleated, his rage ebbing in all but uncontrollably. For a moment he couldn't find words.

Krasnaya said, his voice jittering, "I had some research to do. You see, sir, this . . . this project you and Kardelj started me off on——"

"I had nothing to do with it! It was Kardelj's scheme, confound his idiocy!" Number One all but screamed. "Everything goes wrong at once. His ridiculous scheme to pass the West by teaching our porpoises not only to talk but to read. The fool! The criminal fool. What sort of thing did he have printed on the waterproof plastic paper for them to read? Karl Marx's *Das Kapital!* And now the doubly-damned creatures have organized Soviets and expropriated the herds of whales we had turned over to them for grazing! No! Don't connect me with Kardelj's idiotic schemes!"

"Oh? Well . . . well, I had gathered the opinion that both of you concurred. Anyway, like I say, the project from the first didn't come off quite the way it started. I . . . well . . . we, were thinking in terms of finding out why waiters were surly, why workers and professionals and even officials all tried to, uh, beat the rap, pass the buck, look out for themselves and the devil the hindmost, and all those Americanisms that Kardelj is always using."

Zorin simmered, but let the other go on. Undoubtedly his police chief, Lazar Jovanovic, was even now tracing the call, and this young traitor would soon be under wraps where he could do no more damage to the economy of the Soviet Complex.

"But, well, I found it wasn't just a matter of waiters, and truck drivers and such. It . . . well . . . ran all the way from top to bottom. So, I finally felt as though I was sort of butting my head against a wall. I thought I better start at . . . kind of . . . fundamentals, so I began researching the manner in which the governments of the West handled some of these matters."

"Ah," Zorin said as smoothly as he was able to get out. "Ah. And?" This fool was hanging himself.

The younger man frowned in unhappy puzzlement. "Frankly, I was surprised. I have, of course, read Western propaganda while I worked for *Pravda* in Greater Washington and to the extent I could get hold of it in Moscow, and listened to the Voice of the West on the wireless. I was also, obviously, familiar with our own propaganda. Frankly . . . well . . . I had reserved my opinion in both cases."

This in itself was treason, but Number One managed to get out, almost encouragingly, "What are you driving at, Frol Krasnaya?"

"I found in one Western country that the government was actually paying its peasants, that is, farmers, not to plant crops. The same government subsidized other crops, keeping the prices up to the point where they were hard put to compete on the international markets."

Young Krasnaya frowned, as though in puzzlement. "In other countries, in South America for instance, where the standard of living is possibly the lowest in the West and they need funds desperately to develop themselves, the governments build up large armies, although few of them have had any sort of warfare at all for over a century."

"What is all this about?" Number One growled. Surely, Lazar Jovanovic was on the idiot traitor's trail by now.

Frol took a deep breath and hurried on nervously. "They've got other contradictions that seem unbelievable. For instance, their steel industry will be running at half capacity, in spite of the fact that millions of their citizens have unfulfilled needs, involving steel. Things like cars, refrigerators, stoves. In fact, in their current depression, they'll actually close down perfectly good, modern factories, and throw their people out of employment, at the very time that there are millions of people who need the factory's product."

Frol said reasonably, "Why, sir, I've come to the conclusion that the West has some of the same problems we have. And the main one is politicians."

"What? What do you mean?"

"Just that," Frol said with dogged glumness. "I . . . well, I don't know about the old days. A hundred, even fifty years ago, but as society has become more complicated, more intricate, I simply don't think politicians are capable of directing it. The main problems are those of production and distribution of all the things our science and industry have learned to turn out. And politicians, all over the world, seem to foul it up."

Andrei Zorin growled ominously, "Are you suggesting that I am incompetent to direct the Soviet Complex?"

"Yes, sir," Frol said brightly, as though the other had encouraged him. "That's what I mean. You or any other politician. Industry should be run by trained, competent technicians, scientists, industrialists—and to some extent, maybe, by the consumers—but not by politicians. By definition, politicians know about politics, not industry. But somehow, in the modern world, governments seem to be taking over the running of industry and even agriculture. They aren't doing such a good job, sir."

Zorin finally exploded. "Where are you calling from, Krasnaya?" he demanded. "You're under arrest!"

Frol Krasnaya cleared his throat, apologetically. "No, sir," he said. "Remember? I'm the average Soviet citizen. And it is to be assumed I'd, well . . . react the way any other would. The difference is, I had the opportunity. I'm in Switzerland."

"Switzerland!" Number One roared. "You've defected. I knew you were a traitor, Krasnaya. Like father, like son! A true Soviet would remain in his country and help it along the road to the future."

The younger man looked worried. "Well, yes, sir," he said. "I thought about that. But I think I've done about as much as I could accomplish. You see, these last few months, protected by those 'can do no wrong' credentials, I've been spreading this message around among all the engineers, technicians, professionals, all the more trained, competent people in the Soviet Complex. You'd be surprised how they took to it. I think it's kind of . . . well, snowballing. I mean the idea that politicians aren't capable of running industry. That if the Soviet Republics are to ever get anywhere, some changes are going to have to be made."

Number One could no more than glare.

Frol Krasnaya rubbed his nose nervously, and said, in the way of uneasy farewell, "I just thought it was only fair for me to call you and give a final report. After all, I didn't start all this. It wasn't me who originated the situation. It was you and Kardelj who gave me my chance. I just . . . well . . . expedited things." His face faded from the screen, still apologetic of expression.

Andrei Zorin sat there for a long time, staring at the now dark instrument.

It was in the middle of the night, when the knock came at the door. But then, Andrei Zorin had always thought it would . . . finally.

Chapter Twenty

Weigand Patrick was seeking a moment of refuge in his west wing office. Slumped in his swivel chair, a half-consumed highball in his hand, he eyed the Tri-Di set emptily.

Senator Dethwish was being interviewed by a newsman:

". . . now Senator, this new proposal that the Congress consider giving the country back to what remains of the Indian tribes. I understand it's one of your pet projects."

The senator was obviously indignant. "Well, what about it?"

"I understand the Indians are proving cagey. As that spokesman of theirs, Chief Chicken Little, put it, after what the white man has done to the country——"

"See here," the Senator broke in heatedly, "If the Indians don't like this country they can go back to where. . . ."

"Yes?" the reporter urged.

"No, come to think of it, they can't."

Weigand groaned, and flicked the set off, just as a knock came at the door.

Steve Hammond stuck his head in Weigand Patrick's office door warily. "Mr. Patrick, you know that inventor, the one you sent us with down to Dry Tortugas?"

"How could I forget him?" Weigand Patrick growled.

"Well, he's here again."

"Here again! Well, throw him out!"

"Yes, sir." The head disappeared.

"Hey, wait a minute," Weigand yelled. He finished his drink and put the glass down.

The head came back.

Weigand thought about it. He sighed.

"What does he want?"

Steve Hammond looked blank. "I don't know."

"All right, damn it. Send him in. But listen . . ."

"Yes, sir."

"You stand right outside that door, just in case."

"Yes, sir." Steve Hammond's head disappeared again.

The scrawny beard still looked as though it could use a dosage of mothballs, and the facial expression was still that of a lost pup. But Weigand Patrick was not thrown off guard, this time.

He said, "Sit down Mr. Brown."

The other perched on the edge of a straight chair, and bobbed his Adam's apple. "My friends call me Newt."

Patrick glared at him. "Name one."

Newt Brown considered that for a moment and changed the subject. "I came to you first," he said. When there was no immediate response he went on. "My latest research. I've finally found a use for water."

"Oh, great. What's that got to do with me?"

"It'll solve all the problems that beset the world, Mr. Patrick."

"What are you going to do," Weigand said sarcastically "blow it up?"

"Oh no. Not at all. Just the opposite."

Weigand Patrick said cautiously, "What's the opposite of blowing up the world?"

Newton Brown was obviously launching into his pitch

137

now. "Mr. Patrick, what this world needs is love. Every great thinker in the history of the world has advocated love. Love thy neighbor as thyself was taught long, long before Jesus."

"All right, all right," Weigand said. "Every religious teacher, every philosopher down through the centuries has advocated that we love one another. Man seems to accept the teaching in principle, but when he gets around to dealing with his fellow man, he usually winds up clobbering him, instead."

Newt Brown beamed, as though at a receptive student. "Right," he said.

Weigand Patrick looked at him. "So what are you going to do with water to change all that?"

"Oh, it's not primarily the water. That's just my method of distribution.

"Of what."

"L.A."

Weigand looked at the other for a long moment, wondering if he really wanted to continue this conversation.

Finally, he said, "Los Angeles is already distributed all over hell's half acre. It stretches from San Francisco to San Diego."

"Not Los Angeles—L.A. My new hallucinogen, Love Acid." He hurried on. "We'll dump it in the reservoirs."

"Wait a minute. A new hallucinogen. What's wrong with LSD? Didn't we have enough trouble with the old ones?"

Newt Brown made a scoffing gesture. "LSD, mescaline, psilocybin. Old hat."

"What was that last one?"

"I mean they're antiquated. Nothing. Love Acid is the ultimate hallucinogen. It will solve *all* of the world's problems. No more wars, No more depressions. Everybody will love everybody."

In spite of his caution, Weigand Patrick was becoming intrigued.

"How would it end the depression?"

"What causes depressions? The flow of industry ends. When the owner of an industry cannot make a profit, he closes it down, not caring that there might be thousands of consumers who need the product he manufactures. He doesn't care, though. All he's interested in is making a profit. Now if he *loved* everybody, he wouldn't give a hoot about profit. He'd just want to supply his product to those who needed it."

Weigand Patrick left off consideration of some of the socio-economic ramifications of that, for the time being.

He said, "Now if I get this right, what you want to do is dump this new hallucinogen of yours in the drinking water of the whole country."

"Correct."

"And then everybody would love everybody else?"

"That is correct," Newt Brown beamed.

"Holy smokes."

"Obviously."

"Then, I suppose, after you've dosed everybody in the United States of the Americas, you'll turn it over to Common Europe, the Soviet Complex, and. . . ."

Newt Brown nodded emphatically. "Absolutely. If they refuse the gift, we'll lob it over into their reservoirs by rocket missile. Use up the whole stock pile. We won't want nuclear missiles by that time anyway, we'll *love* everybody, not want to kill them."

"Holy smokes." Weigand Patrick shook his head, momentarily overwhelmed. Something came to him and he narrowed his eyes at the other. "How do I know it works?"

"Oh, it works all right, all right. I've tried it out on all sorts that supposedly hate each other, on cats and dogs, on cobras and mongooses, on ferrets and rats. Oh, it works all right."

"You mean it works on *animals* too?"

"I told you. It's universal. It works on everything."

"You mean, I could give a dallop of this stuff to my worst enemy and then he'd love me?"

Newt Brown was uncomfortable. "Well, admittedly, that's the one shortcoming."

Weigand Patrick looked at him.

Newt Brown squirmed in his chair unhappily. He said, "I assume your worst enemy is a man?"

That didn't quite come through. "Of course."

Newt Brown said grudgingly, "Then, yes. I'm afraid so."

"You're afraid what?"

"He'd want to love you."

A suspicion was beginning to dawn in Weigand Patrick. "Look here," he growled. "When you say that everybody would love everybody, after taking this L.A. of yours, how do you mean——"

"Love, love," Newt Brown said impatiently. "You know what love is."

"There is love and love," Patrick said dangerously. "I love the President's private secretary. I also love my country, and chocolate cake with vanilla ice cream. I also love a parade, but I've never wanted to go to bed with one."

Newt Brown bobbed his adam's apple. "This is the kind of love you undoubtedly feel for the President's secretary."

Weigand stared at him. "You mean this L.A. of yours that you want to slip into the nation's drinking water is a universal aphrodisiac?"

"You might put it that way. I prefer to think——"

"And this Mickey Finn to end all Mickey Finns would give everybody——"

"Everything, not just everybody," Newt Brown injected.

". . . hot pants?"

The self-proclaimed inventor summoned his dignity. "That is not the way I would explain it."

Weigand Patrick yelled, "Hammond!"

Steve Hammond burst into the office, .38 Magnum revolver at the ready.

Newt Brown winced.

"Yes, sir," the Secret Service bodyguard snapped.

"Do they still have chains?"

Steve Hammond looked at him blankly. "Chains, Mr. Patrick?"

"In the old days, the king, or whoever, would yell, *thrown him in chains.*"

Squealing terror, Newt Brown tried to scurry toward the door, but Steve Hammond had him in an arm lock.

Holding the still mewling inventor, with one hand, he turned back to Weigand Patrick. "Well, no sir, I don't think so. All we've got now is handcuffs and leg irons."

"Okay. Get him into handcuffs and leg irons, and into some top security cell."

"Yes sir," Steve Hammond thought about it for a moment. "What's the charge?"

"Charge?"

The bodyguard was apologetic. "Well, yes sir. There ought to be some charge." He added, "Don't you think?"

"Get him into handcuffs and leg irons. I'll put the Department of Justice on it. They ought to be able to figure out something."

When Newton Brown and his escort were gone, Weigand Patrick snapped on his phone screen, growling, "Love thy neighbor, yet."

141

The girl on the White House switchboard said, "I beg your pardon, Mr. Patrick?"

"Get me Rod Watson, over at the Bureau of Statistics. Holy smokes, we've got to find out where this damn depression started, and why."

"Yes sir, that's what I thought you said."

Chapter Twenty-One

Warren Dempsey Witherson's copter-cab floated gently onto the Doolittle Building's landing ramp and bumped to an easy halt.

Automatically, his eyes flicked right and left, while he fiddled in his doublet pocket for a slug. He found it, slipped it into the auto-meter slot, secured his change and opened the cab door.

There were half a dozen pickets, women in shiny corselets, their short swords buckled to their sides. Doctor Witherson ignored the placards they bore and scurried for the lobby, his pince-nez held in hand.

He had a key to the private elevator now and didn't bother to check with the receptionist.

On the top floor, devoted solely to the offices and private quarters of Professor Doolittle himself, he hurried toward the *sanctum* of the motivational research head.

Walthers did no more than look up from his desk and say, "Good morning, Doctor. The Professor is expecting you."

Doctor Witherson mumbled something that wound up with my boy and was past.

The Professor, his calm for once vanished with the

snows of yesteryear, was bellowing at his two-man brain trust.

"The police," he was yelling. "How about the police? A mob can't just storm a Tri-Di station and demolish it!"

Jimmy Leath, who sat at the Professor's desk, a phone held to one ear, said, "Professor, it's a difficult situation. For one thing, this mob isn't a bunch of juvenile delinquents from Harlem or Brooklyn. Some of it's composed of the biggest names in the Blue Book. Besides that, they're all armed with their swords." His eyes went ceilingwards. "I thought those swords were supposed to be decorative, that they weren't meant to take a point or an edge. They seem to be able to chop up doors and furniture with them like they were machetes."

"They *were* only decorative to begin with!" the Professor roared.

Les Frankle said unhappily, "Well, Irene didn't think that was practical so——"

"Irene!" the Professor roared. "Don't ever mention that woman again, Frankle!"

"Yes, sir."

Doctor Witherson, his eyes popping, blatted at Jimmy Leath, "What's happened? I mighta known it. We haven't been cooling off these marks the way we shoulda!"

"Shut up, Kid," the Professor roared. "Confound it, you never were any good in the clutch."

Les said mildly, "Irene says. . . ."

The Professor scowled blood and destruction at him.

Les flushed and went on, "That is, what's really happening is that it's been a long time since women have got up on their high horse about something. It's been almost a century since the temperance movement. And women's suffrage, of course, all came about, so there's been no more suffragettes for as long as anybody can remember."

Jimmy was frowning. "Those that had a cause complex could always go into regular politics."

Les said, "Well, yes, but according to Ire . . . that is, women have never got very far in ordinary politics. They, uh, haven't been able to understand them very well—at least, up until now."

Jimmy Leath, still at the phone, growled, "Neither have men."

The Professor glared at him. "This is no time for levity, James." He spun back to Les. "Go on, confound it. What's happened? You're supposed to be our mass behavior expert."

Les said doggedly, "Well, sir, it was something women could understand. Something they could get riled up about. Being beaten over the head with sales propaganda that had them scrapping their last year's refrigerator because it was white instead of pink. Or changing their perfectly acceptable brand of soap for something twice as expensive, because it was a status symbol, to use a new brand containing super-lanolin. When you hit a woman in the pocketbook, you hit her where it counts."

"SO!" the Professor bellowed.

"Well, sir, all they needed was a banner under which to unite. Something to bring them together in this depression."

"You mean the Joan of Arc fad, you confounded ass!"

"Well, yes sir. You see, the origianl Joan was a reformer. Well, more than that. An actual rebel, according to . . . Well, anyway, she was a non-conformist and revolted against society as she found it. Well, sir, your think tank syndicate, the Oedipus Group, made her the country's ideal. And once the women really got involved in her image they wanted to . . . uh . . . emulate her. So they had to look around for something to rebel against, sir."

Doctor Warren Dempsey Witherson, who had been

taking in only about half of this, spending most of his time and attention at the window, whined, "What's that big crowd gathering down there?"

"Shut up, Kid," the Professor growled. "I got to think."

Jimmy Leath said reasonably, "All the thinking has been done, Professor Doolittle. All the cards are down."

The Professor, his rage ebbing up again pointed a shaking finger at him, then spun and leveled it at Les. "You two. You sold us out. You could have figured this, eight months ago. You're fired, understand!"

"Well, yes sir," Les nodded unhappily. "We kind of figured we would be."

Witherson whined, "Professor, there's a whole mob of marks getting together down there. We better take it on the heel and toe."

The Professor's rage broke. His hands came up, palms upward. "Lads," he said, "How could you do it? You were my team."

Jimmy ran his hand through his hair, uncomfortably. "Not exactly, sir. Like you've said, over and over, you just hired our brains. There wasn't anything ever said about loyalty. When Les first brought up the suggestion about using Joan of Arc as our heroine, we could have given it a whirl, given it a trial run, compiled some sample depth interviews, put it on the computer. In fact, either of us probably could have pretty well guessed what was going to happen—like Les Frankle's wife, Irene, evidently did."

"Then *why*, why, lads, didn't you warn me!"

Les said, as unhappy as his colleague. "Well, it was rather fascinating, the whole thing. You see, you kept talking about the money you paid us and how you were buying our brains, but the fact was we were more interested in observing the working mechanics of your organization than anything else. Fascinating, sir. Absolutely.

145

I'm no engineer, but I continually get a picture of an enormous machine slipping its clutch, or belt, or however they say it, and going wild."

Witherson whimpered, "Professor, they're beginning to stream into the building. They're waving them swords!"

Les walked over to the window beside him and peered down, "There's Irene," he said, shaking his head. "Out in front."

Witherson whirled and caught the Professor's doublet sleeve. "Listen, we gotta get out of here. We're warm! You must have some back way, if I know you, Professor. It's your building, you had it built."

The Professor shook him off.

He said to his ex-brain trust, pleadingly, "Listen, lads, By George. There must be some angle. Some way of rescuing this situation."

Les was shaking his head earnestly. "Well, I don't think so, sir. Jimmy and I put it on the computors last night."

The Professor, now beginning to allow the Funked Out Kid to pull him toward the door, demanded, "Well, how did they ever get rid of that original Saint Joan of. . . ." Then he stopped and his eyes narrowed. "They burnt her at the stake, didn't they?"

Les nodded, and spoke above the roar that suddenly was coming from the outer offices. "Yes, sir. They had to do that to shut her up, sir. And sir, well, I don't think it'll be so easy to burn Irene."

The Professor and the Funked Out Kid had made it down the secret elevator, out the back, and into a copter-cab.

Even as the Professor dialed a destination, with a shaking hand the Kid was whining. "On the lam again. Warm again, after all these years."

146

DEPRESSION OR BUST

"Don't be silly, Kid," The Professor said, with shaky joviality. "We've got enough of a taw stashed away to live happily ever after off in Spain or Switzerland. I've had it all planned for years. A hideout apartment here in town where we can disguise ourselves. A vehicle to take us to the Canadian border. Lots of funds in a safe deposit box to grease our way. We're as safe as in our mother's arms, Kid. Remember, the fuzz isn't after us, just a bunch of hysterical dames. It was all legit, as far as John Law's concerned. You were even in the President's brain trust."

They pulled up before an imposing edifice.

"What's this?" the Kid whined apprehensively.

"Bank. My safe deposit box. We've got practically all the money left in the country. Let's hurry, Kid." The beam had returned to his eye, the pomposity to his manner.

The Funked Out Kid fumbled for a coin, stuck it into the copter-cab's slot and reached for the door handle.

It was then that the cab's lights began flicking red, a siren began to ululate from its hood.

The Funked Out Kid wrenched at the door, which held tight.

And a voice from the cab speaker said, "You are under arrest for utilizing other than legal tender, and face a five year imprisonment for counterfeiting. This is a police decoy cab of the Bureau of Transportation. You will remain seated until an officer of the law has arrived."

The Professor turned a beady eye on the Funked Out Kid who shrank back into the upholstery.

"By *George*," the Professor said.

Chapter Twenty-two

Weigand Patrick, flanked by the two cold-eyed Secret Service men, came up to the cement walk, taking in from the side of his eyes the unkempt condition of the old house's lawn. It wasn't just the lawn. The place could have used a coat of paint—or two. One of the shutters was hanging from a single hinge. There was newspaper stuffed in a broken window.

Patrick grunted. "Place looks better than most, these days."

The others said nothing.

He mounted the wooden steps, which creaked forbiddingly, and knocked on the front door, assuming, without trying, that the bell would be out of order.

An elderly woman peered out at them. She looked like every other elderly woman he had ever seen, all combined. She would have no trouble getting an extra's job as an old lady, in any Tri-Di production Hollywood made—if Hollywood had been making any Tri-Di shows these days. Who could afford to advertise on Tri-Di anymore?

Weigand Patrick said politely, "Is this where Marvin Sellers lives?"

She said immediately, "If you're bill collectors——"

"We know, we know. Mr. Sellers couldn't pay if we were, but we're not."

"You can't get blood out of a turnip," she said.

"A very apt phrase you've coined," he bowed gently.

She turned and yelled over her shoulder, "Marv! Marv!" and then disappeared.

Marv came to the door and looked at them in suspicion. "Yeah?"

Weigand Patrick looked at the other for a long moment.

"So you're the one who started all this," he murmured.

"What?" Marv said suspiciously.

Weigand Patrick said, "Can I talk to you privately?"

"Well, I don't know. Why? I guess so. Come on in." He held the broken-screened door open. "In here's the parlor."

Weigand Patrick and the two Secret Service men followed the bricklayer into the Victorian period living room.

Marv Sellers said, "Sit down, gents. What's all this about?"

Weigand Patrick said tightly, "Boys, this talk has to be absolutely private."

Guns flowed into the hands of the two ultra-trained operatives. One stationed himself to the side of the window, staring out, empty of eye. The other stood at the door, open the mildest of cracks so that he could see into the hall beyond.

"Hey, what the hell's going on?" Marv Sellers protested.

The two Secret Service men ignored him.

"Sit down, Mr. Sellers," Patrick said soothingly, as he reached for his pipe. "I'm a special representative from the President." He brought forth credentials, handed them to the other, and then fumbled for his tobacco pouch.

"Special representative from the President? You mean of the United States?"

"That is correct, Mr. Sellers." Patrick got his pipe going, then brought forth another sheaf of papers. He checked through them, found what he wanted.

"Mr. Sellers, two years ago, on Saturday, May 12th at ten p.m., you phoned the Wilkins Appliances Shop and told them to come get a new deep freeze you had bought shortly before. Mr. Sellers, that action on your part precipitated the current economic slump."

Marv Sellers bug-eyed him. "Who, me?"

"That is correct." Patrick held up a hand. "Yes, yes, I know what you are thinking. That many people send back appliances, cars, every other commodity. And usually this is simply a part of the workings of the economy, part of the give and take of the everyday business scene. However, private enterprise, as a socio-economic system, is a sensitive mechanism. Evidently, ours had been running at a delicate balance. It was your individual unpremeditated act that unleashed tiny forces that became larger forces and still larger, finally leading to the utter collapse of our economy."

"Jesus," Marv Sellers said. "Me?" He thought about it, round eyed. "Wow. I'm surprised the President didn't send the F.B.I. after me."

Patrick said soothingly, "He couldn't have even had he wanted to, Mr. Sellers. He let the F.B.I go last week as part of the government retrenchment. All except Edgar, of course. There were no longer any bankrobbers, there's nothing left in the banks to rob, and the Communists are no longer desirous of taking over the country."

Marv spread his hands. "Well, all I can say is, I'm sorry. There's nothing I can do about it. Here I am, living with my wife's people. No job. Flat broke."

Weigand Patrick was nodding. "It's a top secret, last ditch try. Back in Washington, we've dubbed it Project Sellers. We're up against the wall, Mr. Sellers."

"Project Sellers?" Marv blurted.

"Correct." Weigand Patrick turned his eyes to the Secret Service man at the window. "Steve, let me have that envelope."

"Yes, sir." Steve Hammond brought a long envelope from his inner doublet pocket, brought it over to Patrick and then returned to the window and his guard duties.

Patrick said, "Remember, this is topmost security. Highest priority. Everything would immediately be ruined if it got out. It all must be spontaneous. Not even your wife must know, Mr. Sellers." He handed over the envelope.

"Phoebe? I can't even tell Phoebe?"

"Absolutely no one."

Marv Sellers hesitated, but then, as though hypnotized by a snake, slowly opened the envelope.

And brought forth a thick sheaf of spanking new banknotes.

"What's this?" he said.

"Obviously, money."

Sellers chuckled bitterly. "U.S. Government money?"

Patrick said, "I know, I know. However, there are still sixteen pounds of gold in Fort Knox. This money has been issued based on that."

Sellers was round eyeing him again.

Patrick said hurriedly, "And there'll be more when you've spent that. The President is arranging for a loan from Monaco. It seems that the present Prince of that country has a soft spot for America. His mother was an American, or something."

"All right," Sellers said. "I'm as patriotic as the next one. What do I do?"

Chapter Twenty-three

Phoebe and Marv Sellers and Old Sam moved back into the house on Camino de Palmas the following day. It had never sold, anyway.

Marv was admirably stubborn. He had a government job. He'd tell Phoebe and Old Sam nothing more than that.

The same day, he phoned Barry Benington.

"Mr. Benington," he said. "I've had a change of mind."

"Change in mind? What's that, what's that?" the old man wheezed.

"That car I sold you. You know, I liked that car. I'd like to buy it back."

The old man turned sly. "Why, I don't know about that, Mr. Sellers. I've rather taken to it myself."

Marv said, "I'd be willing to pay you five hundred more than you gave me for the old wreck."

"Five hundred? Well, I don't know. I've had her polished up, you know, spent a lot of money on that beautiful car."

"I'll make it a thousand," Marv said.

"It's a deal!" the oldster wheezed quickly.

That afternoon when Bill Waters came up on his bicycle to deliver some bologna and cheese to old man Benington, the other met him at the kitchen door.

Benington wheezed, "Bill, what's the price of one of them Buick Cayuses?"

Bill Waters looked at him. "I thought you bought yourself a used car, Mr. Benington."

"Yeah, but I'm tired of it. Sold it back. I always did kinda hanker after one of them air-cushion cars. Can you still get me one?"

Bill Waters felt a tremor. He said, trying to keep his voice even, "Well, I sort of closed up my place. But, come to think of it, I guess I've still got the franchise. I could certainly order one from the distributor in Denver."

"Now, you do that for me, Bill. I've got the cash money right here for a down payment."

Some of Bill Waters elan, long submerged, surfaced. He gushed, "Mr. Benington, you'll love these new model cars. I understand they're built so low you have to enter them through a manhole."

Marv Sellers was saying to Jim Wilkins, "Yep, what we need is one of them new deep freezes. Phoebe wants one of them cerise models."

Wilkins was taken aback. "You got the down payment, Mr. Sellers?"

"Thought I'd just pay cash."

"I can sure as hell order you one. We don't have any demonstrators in stock. The shop's closed."

"That's all right. I'll pay you now. And look, Jim. The other day, I was reading about a nuclear Martini stirrer. Has a little atomic pack in it, like. Stir your Martinis for twenty years, before running down. Now a gadget like that——"

Jim Wilkins said quickly, "I know where I can order you one. I'll get several of them. You know, it's about time I opened up that shop of mine again."

"Sure is," Marv said.

When Norman Foxbeater drove past the *Lovee Dovee Hottee Doggee Shoppee* he was mildly surprised to find the place hadn't folded its doors. In fact, it seemed to be having quite a play.

Whatever brought him to enter, he couldn't say. Possibly it was becuse it was so unusual to see even mild business.

He sat in a small booth and allowed the waitress to bring him a dish of very small weiners, a portion of baked beans and some potato salad. The baked beans were fabaulous.

He recognized a few of the faces. Over there was a

153

bricklayer who had once worked briefly for the Foxbeaters in the building of a backyard barbeque. What was his name? Sellers or something. And over there was Barry Benington, who'd once had an account with Foxbeater and Fodor. And on the other side of the room was Bill Waters and his wife. When times had been better, Bill had belonged to the country club. Foxbeater nodded to him and received a cheerful wave in return.

Hmmm. Things were evidently looking up for Bill Waters.

Mrs. Perriwinkle came sailing by, all smiles, a dish of her tiny hot dogs in hand.

She recognized him and came to a halt.

Foxbeater said, "You seem to be doing quite a business, Mrs. Perriwinkle."

"Oh," she lied airily, "it's always like this. If the truth be known, one of these days I'll be dropping by to put some of my earnings back into Mutual Funds." She swept on.

He looked after her.

An hour later he came into Mortimer Fodor's office.

"Mortimer," he said thoughtfully, "my instinct tells me it's time to pull that money out of Switzerland and invest in American securities."

His senior partner looked at him. "Oh? Well, good. Get this all ironed out and I'll be able to retire. I'll bet I can get a yacht built for a pittance these days."

"Ummmm," Foxbeater nodded. "But don't put it off too long. Get your order in while things are still slow."

They were seated around the kitchen table.

Phoebe said, "Guess what? Mr. Edwards wants me to come back to work. They've got a whole batch of new gadgets they're going to market."

Marv said, "Oh? Such as what?"

"Oh, a whole lot of things. When everybody was out of work a lot of these technicians and inventors and all didn't have anything else to do so they kind of puttered around in their cellar and garage workshops and laboratories and came up with just about everything. Like the electric spoons. There's a little stud on the side. You can switch it all the way over from stirring your coffee to eating soup."

Marv said, "Well, I've got news too. Heard from my old boss. He's going to be constructing a new factory. Place where they'll be manufacturing air-cushion roller skates."

Old Sam groaned. "Back to the rat race," he said. "I knew it wouldn't last. They ain't making them like they used to. In the old days, a depression was good to last for nigh onta ten years."

"Knock it off, Gramps," Marv growled at him.

The old boy came to his feet. "I better put away that apple sign of mine fer future reference. I'll bet the next one will be a doozy."

Chapter Twenty-four

"Yes, sir," Weigand Patrick said, with satisfaction. "It worked."

The President was jubilant.

He rubbed his hands together. He chortled, "Now we can get back to my Far-Out Society. And we can get that police action down in the Antarctic going again. Scotty, get me Admiral Pennington, on the phone. We're going to take him out of mothballs. And instruct the Octagon to discontinue melting down the Fifteenth Fleet."

"Yes, Mr. President," Scotty said.

"And Scotty, take a letter to those Porpoise Union smart alecs. Tell them that their request for human children to experiment with, to teach them the porpoise language, is out of the question. Ah, think of some good excuse. We've got to keep those whales coming, now people will be able to afford meat again. Ah, tell them that human kids have a hard time breathing under water, or something." He tapped the side of his nose slyly.

"Yes, Mr. President," Scotty said.

The President added thoughtfully, "I wonder how those boys up on the moon are doing."

"Well, sir," Weigand said, "That's going to be one of your first problems, now that the depression is over. It seems that at the same time we deserted our moonbase, and raised that monument to the space heroes, the Russkies also were running out of cash, and abandoned theirs. So the two bases evidently got together, merged their resources, the hydroponic tanks they get their food from, and such, and proclaimed the Republic of Luna. They've taken over all the TV and Communications relay stations, and are making some pretty stiff demands about rates before any Earth governments can use the services."

"What!" the Chief Executive yelled. "They can't do that to us, the ingrates! I'll liberate them!"

Chapter Twenty-five

Weigand Patrick flicked on the phone screen and growled, "Yes, what is it?"

It was Scotty. She said, "Listen, I want you to do me a favor."

"I'd climb the highest mountain, I'd swim the deepest river——"

"Great. I'm at my apartment. Look, I left a report on my desk. What's the chances of bringing it over?"

"What do you think I am, a delivery boy?" he wailed. "I'm busy. That Oedipus Group, the think tank outfit, they've fouled up the women's vote something awful. I've got to——"

"Please, the report's very . . . confidential. I wouldn't want anyone else to see it."

"All right, all right. I'll be over."

He flicked the phone screen switch off, muttering, got up and headed in the direction of her office.

He rang the bell, pushed at the door, found it ajar, and entered.

He was scowling, as he closed the door behind him, "Scotty," he called. "Come and get this damn report, I've got to get back to the office."

She came quickly from behind the door, grabbed him in a judo hold.

"Hey!" Weigand Patrick yelled.

He felt himself flying through the air, his arms and legs going every which way.

"Iley!" he yelled, landing flat on his back on the bed, the covers of which had been turned down neatly.

Scotty stood over him, a wicked gleam in her eyes, even as she began to unbutton her dress.

"No, look," he said desperately. "I've got a press conference waiting."

"Let it wait," she growled.

www.ingramcontent.com/pod-product-compliance
Lightning Source LLC
Chambersburg PA
CBHW020648180626
46816CB00003B/1175